THE CENTRAL SCHOOL OF SPEECH AND DRAMA

UNIVERSITY OF LONDON

Please return or renew this item by the last date shown.

**The Library, Central School of Speech and Drama,
Embassy Theatre, Eton Avenue, London, NW3 3HY
http://heritage.cssd.ac.uk
library@cssd.ac.uk
Direct line: 0207 559 3942**

THE
WHITE NIGHTS
OF
ST PETERSBURG

Geoffrey Trease

PIPER
PAN MACMILLAN
CHILDREN'S BOOKS

First published 1967 by Macmillan & Co Ltd

This revised edition published 1994
by Pan Macmillan Children's Books
a division of Pan Macmillan Publishers Limited
Cavaye Place London SW10 9PG
and Basingstoke

Associated companies throughout the world

ISBN 0 330 33423 9

1 3 5 7 9 8 6 4 2

A CIP catalogue record for this book is available from
the British Library

Phototypeset by Intype, London
Printed by Cox & Wyman Ltd, Reading, Berkshire

Contents

CHAPTER ONE

City in the Mist

The mist ... It swirled everywhere ... Except under the high roof of the Finland Station, where the yellow glare of all those lights just managed to keep it at bay.

The train hissed and wheezed to a standstill. This was it, then. The end of the seemingly endless journey, the start of the next phase, the real adventure ...

His fellow-passengers, a Swedish couple and a Finn, grunted their farewells in broken English and were gone. Burly porters invaded the compartment, bearded, fur-capped, white-aproned. Dave saw his own bags seized. He followed anxiously and was relieved to find, as he jumped down from the yellow second-class coach, that the giant who had borne them away was standing there on the platform.

'Taxi, barin?'

Dave hesitated. A taxi was no good if he didn't know where he was going. There should have been someone to meet him. His father had said, 'some guy from the Embassy'. Dave looked round. There seemed to be thousands of people in the echoing terminus, not one of them interested in his arrival. Soldiers with rolled blankets and slung rifles, peasants in smelly sheepskin with mysterious bundles, kerchiefed old women like round wooden dolls, elegant gentlemen with neat beards and *pince-nez* and astrakhan collars, ladies swathed in furs and exuding waves of French scent, haughty-looking officers, so exquisitely tailored and tight-waisted it must be true that they wore corsets as people said . . .

He was relieved when a cultured Bostonian voice spoke in his ear.

'David Hopkins?'

He swung round. A young man in a soft hat and overcoat of London cut thrust out a welcoming hand.

'I'm Wallace Hayes. From the Embassy. You had me worried for a while.'

'Sorry, sir. I reckon the train was late. It broke down or something.'

'Everything breaks down in this country. All the time,' said Mr Hayes languidly. 'One expects that. But I was afraid you weren't on it. I waited *here*.' He indicated the blue first-class coach that they were now passing as they followed the porter towards the exit. There was a hint of rebuke in his voice. 'It never occurred to me to stand by the second-class!'

Dave muttered another apology. He was beginning to get a very definite feeling about this drawling young diplomat, but just now, amid all this bizarre, faintly-scaring Russian strangeness, he was thankful for any fellow-countryman. He comforted himself by remembering that last talk with his father in New York. Now, son, David Hopkins Senior had said, I've asked the Ambassador as a personal favour to me to make sure you get settled in O.K. But don't let those other guys at the Embassy get you rattled with their fancy talk. We could most likely buy up the whole bunch if we wanted.

Aloud, Dave said: 'I changed to second-class when I

reached Helsingfors. Dad said to mix with ordinary folk and get to figure out the way they live.'

'I suppose you have to – in business.'

Mr Hayes' tone was as chilly as the night they stepped into as they passed out of the station lights.

A dank fog slapped their cheeks. It wavered like a drab gauze curtain, veiling the empty vastness of a square that Dave felt rather than saw, stretching flatly away into the night. Here the lamps were blurred into sickly yellow blotches. He could just make out the last of the taxis moving off, and, yes – that must be a real droshky, with shaggy horse and shaggier driver, jingling away piled high with baggage.

'Here's the car,' said Mr Hayes.

Dave climbed into the back with him and was cheered to see, over the shoulder of the uniformed chauffeur, the tiny Stars and Stripes flicking and straining on the bonnet.

It was good to see Old Glory in this outlandish place.

Where were they driving? Where *was* this city anyhow, this famous St Petersburg, this capital from which one man, Tsar Nicholas, ruled an empire covering a sixth of the whole earth?

The Ford nosed its way cautiously forward into the whiteness. Skeins of mist smoked across the headlamp beams. Straining his eyes to left and right Dave could see no loom of buildings, no hint of lighted windows. Only, at intervals, the pallid stain of street-lamps, battling hopelessly with the fog. There was a tang in his nostrils, partly of wood fires and partly of the sea.

Mr Hayes sensed his puzzlement. 'We're crossing the Alexander Bridge.'

'Over the River Neva?'

'That's right.'

'Must be wide!'

The bridge seemed to go on for ever. Once the mist thinned to give a glimpse of parapet. Then it came boiling over again, as though from some giant cauldron beneath the balustrade.

'It's still the one river here,' Mr Hayes explained. 'Before it splits into the different channels. The city's all islands and canals. Like Venice. You'll see, tomorrow.'

'You sure can't see much tonight!'

'I'm told it's often this way in the fall. You get a westerly, and this white mist rolls in from the Gulf of Finland.'

'This what they call the White Nights, sir?'

'Goodness, no!' Mr Hayes gave a superior little snicker. 'The White Nights are beautiful – you get them at midsummer. Petersburg being so near the Arctic Circle – almost the same latitude as Alaska—'

'The Midnight Sun!'

'Not quite. But very near.'

'I'd like to see that.'

There were buildings now, and more lights, but fuzzy and shapeless. The car swung slowly to the right. The headlamps caught a line of hunched, fur-capped pedestrians, surprised and scrambling for the sidewalk. A string of street-cars brought a sudden passing brilliance, after which the fog seemed drabber and woollier than before.

'We're in the main street. The Nevsky Prospect. It's nearly three miles long!'

'Some street!'

Another glimpse of figures, motionless these, standing in line outside a blankly shuttered store.

'A bread queue,' said Mr Hayes. He seemed to like British words as much as British tailoring.

4

'Queue?' Dave echoed the unfamiliar expression.

'They're waiting for the bakery to open tomorrow morning.'

'Gee! I didn't know things were that bad.'

'Don't worry. We'll see you don't starve.'

Dave bristled. 'I didn't mean that, sir.'

Mr Hayes seemed not to notice his irritation. By dawn, he said, there would be long queues everywhere. For bread, sugar, tobacco, anything that was going . . .

'But not much *is* going. Remember, the Russians have been fighting the Germans since 1914 – and getting the worst of it. Two years of defeat and disaster! Not the best time for a boy your age to—'

'I'll be O.K., sir. Dad wants me to stand on my own feet. And he takes the long view about Russia. Reckons it's a country with a future.' Dave tried to speak with grave confidence, like the solid businessman his father wanted him to become.

'He may be right,' said Mr Hayes politely. For *he* was aiming to become a successful diplomat, and this boy was the son of a man who mattered. 'We turn off here,' he went on. 'We've fixed up a room for you at the Pension Yalta. Kind of boarding house, very respectable.'

'Thank you, sir.'

'Madame Mitrova speaks English, but you can practise your Russian on the others.'

'Fine. That's the way Dad wants it.'

The car stopped, crawled forward again, came to a final standstill. The chauffeur climbed out and waved a torch to right and left. Dave saw massive doorways. On the other side, iron railings greasy with mist, a shimmer of golden light on black water.

'The Fontanka,' Mr Hayes explained. 'One of the

canals. Ah, he's found the number. I'll go up with you and make the introductions.'

'Thank you, sir.'

'After that, you're on your own.'

'Sure.'

'Mind you,' Mr Hayes continued, lowering his voice as they got out, 'you must come to us if you're in any serious difficulty. But do watch your step. This isn't America. Especially politics. I guess you're a bit young to bother with them. The kids here are different. They go crazy.'

'I'll stay out of trouble, sir.'

Dave's father had never told him he was 'a bit young'. At sixteen, Dad said, a boy should be ready to get up and go. He'd founded his own business when he was that age.

They stood on the doorstep. The chauffeur brought the bags. 'Anything you want to ask?' said Mr Hayes.

'Only—' Dave began and stopped.

'Yes?'

'No, it's nothing, sir. It doesn't matter.'

It seemed silly at this moment, late at night and in the depths of the fog, to ask how to get to Zubova Street. Also, Mr Hayes would want to know why.

Some instinct checked the words on his lips. Better perhaps not to tell the smooth, superior young gentleman from the Embassy about the girl who had spoken to him in the corridor of the Stockholm hotel, or about the package lying snugly between the folded shirts in his suitcase.

Luckily, before Mr Hayes could ask anything more, there was a squeak of hinges and they turned to face a peering figure silhouetted in the doorway. Behind, dimly lit, a staircase twisted out of sight.

There was a brief exchange in Russian between the chauffeur and the man who had opened the door. Then the man took over the bags, sketched a cringing kind of bow, and led the way upstairs. Mr Hayes followed with Dave. It was not an inviting kind of entrance, Dave thought. There was a mustiness, and a whiff of something worse. Nor did he much fancy the man carrying his bags. He had lank grey hair, straggling from under a filthy peaked cap, and, when he turned and looked down to make sure that they were following, he had shifty eyes.

'This is the *dvornik*,' Mr Hayes murmured, as if he felt that some explanation was called for.

'The—?'

'The *dvornik*. Kind of janitor.'

'Oh. I see.'

'He looks after the whole building – Madame Mitrova only rents the top two floors. Every building in the city has one of these men. He sweeps the yard, chops logs, does all the chores. He'll take your passport to the police tomorrow and fix your residential permit. You tip him a rouble for that.'

'I'll remember.'

The janitor was halfway up the next flight of stairs.

'Not that it's any extra trouble for him,' said Mr Hayes. 'He has to visit the police-station every morning anyway, to turn in his report.'

'Report, sir?'

'Sh! Not that he's likely to know any English! He keeps an eye on what goes on here. Suspicious visitors, late-night comings and goings, anything the authorities might like to hear about.'

'Holy smoke! You mean – he's a kind of police spy?'

'So is every *dvornik* in St Petersburg.'

'Holy smoke!' said Dave again. He could think of no adequate comment, which was lucky, because they had caught up with the janitor, who had set down the bags outside a pair of tall double doors and was pressing the bell.

'This isn't America, you know,' said Mr Hayes gently.

'I guess not,' said Dave.

CHAPTER TWO

Seven Round a Samovar

It was like waking from a gloomy dream, after that blind drive through the city and the climb upstairs behind the faintly sinister janitor, to step suddenly into the warm brightness of the Pension Yalta.

'I leave you in good hands,' said Mr Hayes. 'Goodnight, Madame Mitrova!' He backed out, obviously glad to have finished a tiresome duty.

Madame was a trim little woman, so light on her feet she almost floated across the hallway. Her wrinkled face was like carved ivory, her eyes bright as a soldier's buttons. She chattered English with an odd accent, hard to follow. From behind an inner door throbbed a hilarious rumpus – a piano was tinkling, someone was twangling another instrument, a banjo maybe, and there was singing and laughter.

A maid-servant, even older than Madame, took Dave's overcoat and cap. Madame put one hand on his arm with a reassuring squeeze. The other, white, delicate and glitteringly be-ringed, she laid on the knob of the inner door, which she flung open with a theatrical gesture.

'Ladies and gentlemen! May I present our new guest? Mr David Hopkins – from New York!'

The hubbub died. Flushed and feeling rather foolish, Dave let himself be steered into the long living-room. It was only afterwards, when alone with time on his hands, that he took in the details of the room that was to be the centre of his life for the next twelve months – the great stove with the log-fire rumbling inside its belly, the walls covered with signed photographs of dancers or bold crayon sketches for stage costumes Madame Mitrova had worn long ago, the sacred ikon in one corner with the tiny lamp winking in front of it, the books and papers strewn everywhere, the pot-plants and the lace curtains and the bobbly-fringed table-cloth, the portraits of the bearded Tsar and his cousin, so very like him, King George the Fifth of England.

That first evening he could not spare eyes for photographs. There were too many living faces turned to smile at him, too many welcoming voices to answer, too many names to remember.

'Another for the mad-house!' cried a snub-nosed girl of his own age. She looked – and sounded – absolutely British. Tall like himself, fresh-faced, might have been pretty, but what had she done to her hair? It was bright chestnut, beautiful, only it was hacked short, as if she'd gone for it herself with garden shears or something.

'Miss Rosalind Lowdham,' said Madame. 'But I should present you in due order – to your elders first.' And she led Dave to the table, where a bony, wispy old woman was sitting in front of a child's game, rattling the dice and apparently playing against herself. 'Miss Upton,' murmured Madame. Not *more* British, thought Dave despairingly. When was he going to learn Russian?

Miss Upton threw the dice, moved a yellow counter five places round the board, and offered him her hand.

'How do you do, Mr Hopkins?' She looked up at him with pale watery eyes. She wore a black velvet band round her throat and spoke with genteel precision. 'Madame was quite correct to present you first to Miss Lowdham. For she is the *Honourable* Rosalind Lowdham – ' The old lady held the word in her mouth for a moment, enjoying it like a soft-centred chocolate. 'Her father, of course, is Lord Tintern. So, whatever her age, Miss Lowdham would always take precedence of little me.'

'Miss Upton!' protested the girl with a scowl of mock anger, brandishing a book as if about to throw it.

All this 'Lord' and 'Honourable' stuff was so much Greek to Dave. 'Glad to know you, ma'am,' he said politely.

Miss Upton seized the dice again, then seemed struck by a sudden thought. 'I hope, young man, you have brought some lump sugar?'

He stared down into those faded eyes. They had taken on an eager, almost piggy look. 'Lump sugar? Why, no—'

'What a pity! Someone should have told you. To come such a long, dangerous journey – all those dreadful mines and submarines – and not bring sugar! What a wasted opportunity!'

'Gee, I'm sorry—'

But Miss Upton had returned to her game and was pushing a red counter rapidly round the board to overtake a blue. Madame Mitrova hurriedly went on with the introductions.

The other three people were all Russian. Dave was relieved about that, thinking of the letter he would have to write to his father, though for his own sake he was relieved to find that they all spoke some English.

Sonya Mitrova didn't say much at all. She just smiled from her perch on the piano stool. She was a dancer, it seemed, as her grandmother had been. In her, across the gulf of half a century, the same petite figure and graceful movements were reproduced. But Sonya's pale, oval face was unlined, her smooth hair black as best coal instead of ashen grey.

Anton Korolenko had been strumming the balalaika. He was a lanky youth, sallow, with a big nose, intense eyes, and a shock of coarse dark hair flaring up from his high temples like a horse's mane. He rushed impulsively across the room, bumping into a chair, and wrung Dave's hand, babbling something about America being the land of freedom. As he was studying English at the University his fluency was not so surprising.

Finally, there was Mr Zorin, middle-aged, burly, and double-chinned, with a heavy moustache. He sat puffing at a curved pipe, slyly twinkling behind his spectacles. He grunted cordially enough, and shook Dave's hand, but did not contribute much to the conversation.

'Now it is time for our tea,' announced Madame. 'Come to the table, everybody.' She waved her new guest to the chair at her side. 'And what,' she inquired, 'is your father's name?'

Dave blinked uncertainly. 'Why,' he stammered foolishly, 'the same as mine – Hopkins.' He wondered why they all burst out laughing.

'Madame means his first name,' said the Honourable, as Dave privately labelled her.

'Oh, I get it! Well, that's the same as mine too. He's David Hopkins Senior.'

'Then,' said Madame, 'we shall call you David Davidovitch – David the son of David. That is our Russian custom. The first name by itself is for the family and intimate friends. The surname – ' she made a comical face – 'is for Government forms and strangers and such like. But in polite society you are David Davidovitch.' She pointed round the table, giving them all their other names. Dave made a mental note that the pretty grand-daughter must be addressed as Sonya Pavlovna and the gangling student as Anton Ilyitch. No one suggested that he should call Miss Upton anything but Miss Upton, or Madame anything but Madame. And Mr Zorin seemed to remain Mr Zorin to everybody but Madame, who alone called him Josef Andreievitch. As for the Honourable Rosalind Lowdham, it had been worked out that she was Linda Ivanovna, because Lord Tintern's name was John, but Dave could not imagine himself ever using that form.

What a complicated country! What with a different alphabet, and all this name business, you were all mixed up before you even started the language itself! Masculine and feminine endings too . . . Madame's late lamented husband had been Mitrov not Mitrova – and if Dave had brought his kid sister with him (God forbid) they'd have wanted to call her Sadie Davidovna instead of Davidovitch like himself.

Aw, I give up, he thought. But he knew quite well he wouldn't. He'd lick this darned language, then there'd be one thing in the world he could do that Dad couldn't.

Madame began to pour the tea.

The pot looked tiny for seven people, but he noticed that she continually refilled it with boiling water from the samovar, a gleaming copper urn that stood on the table beside her. It had a small grate in the bottom, burning charcoal, and a chimney going up through the centre so that the water kept gently sizzling all the time. There was neither milk nor lemon. Both were almost unobtainable in St Petersburg because of the war. Those who liked sugar brought out their own rations, treasured separately in tins or boxes. They pressed Dave to help himself, though Miss Upton did not press him very hard.

'I never take sugar with tea,' he insisted. Which was sort of true, he told himself, because he never drank tea back home at all, only coffee. He'd have to learn to, now. The tea scalded his lips and was so weak it didn't taste very different from boiling water. But there was a smoky fragrance in the steam, strangely agreeable.

'When are you Americans coming into the war?' the English girl demanded.

'I guess it's only a matter of time.' Dave was faithfully echoing his father, but he hoped she wouldn't try to pin him down to further explanations.

It was the student, Anton, who broke in: 'How can you? I read in the newspaper, your President Wilson says that the United States will remain neutral. His opponents say the same. You are a democracy, you do what the most people wish – so I cannot understand—'

'I don't know much about politics,' said Dave nervously.

'And Anton knows nothing else,' said Sonya with a smile that was mocking yet affectionate. 'Always he talks of politics!'

'But tonight we shall not,' her grandmother decided. 'Our guest is tired from his journey. Let us forget the war!'

They talked of other things. Bit by bit, Dave learnt about his fellow-guests and what they were doing there. The puzzling presence of the Honourable Rosalind was explained. There was an Anglo-Russian Hospital in St Petersburg, staffed by British doctors and nurses, directed by Lady Sybil Grey, and housed in the palace of the Grand Duke Dimitri. Rosalind had run away from her boarding school in England, falsified her age, and wangled herself into the party. Lady Sybil had been furious at first, but too good a sport to send her back, especially as the journey was dangerous.

'So she said I could stay and make myself useful. But she won't have me living in the hospital and breaking regulations, so I have a room here at Madame's.'

'But your mother—' said Dave, aghast but admiring. 'Wasn't she mad at you, running off like that?'

'Mummy couldn't say much, could she? I mean, when I was a child, she spent half her time in prison—'

'*Prison?*' Dave echoed, his hair almost standing on end.

'Suffragettes, you know. Don't you have them? Demanding votes for women and all that. Mummy was always breaking up meetings. She broke shop-windows too – she had an immense handbag, she could put a hammer in it. Once she chained herself to the Prime Minister's railings in Downing Street—'

'Holy smoke!'

'She's suspended operations now and thrown herself into the war effort. So she can hardly complain if I do as well. Incidentally,' the girl added cheerfully, 'if you're wondering about my hair—'

'N-no,' he lied.

'You must be. It's a ghastly mess, I know. I cut it myself. You see, these poor Russian soldiers are brought into the hospital in such a state, and I can stand most things, but the thought of getting *lice*—'

'Shall we change the subject?' interrupted Miss Upton.

Dave was not surprised to learn that she was a retired governess. She had spent most of her life with various princely families in Russia. When about to return to England, she had been caught by the outbreak of war and was stuck in St Petersburg, living on her annuity, until it should be safe to cross the sea.

'I am glad to know that you at least have come here with your parents' approval,' she told Dave, with a sideways look at the Honourable Rosalind, 'although I don't know why your father should wish you to learn Russian. I have lived here for thirty years and I have never needed more than a few words.'

'Really, ma'am? But how—'

'In the Grand Duke's household,' said Miss Upton impressively, 'we always spoke French or English. Russian was for the servants.'

Anton looked as if he were going to burst. 'Miss Upton!' he protested. 'Russian is the language of Tolstoy – of Pushkin, Dostoevsky, Turgenev, Chekhov—'

'And of Anton Ilyitch Korolenko,' said Sonya with the same quiet kindly mockery as before, 'and he uses more of it than all of them put together.'

The student subsided for the time being. He sat there rather like the samovar, gently simmering. It was not long before he boiled over again.

Mr Zorin, speaking in slow, guttural, carefully chosen English, asked why Dave's father took such an interest in a backward country like Russia.

'I guess he thinks it has great possibilities, sir. But he reckons it needs more foreign capital. Once this war is over, he'd like to get his foot in the door here. There's a lot of money to be made. They say labour's cheap here, and it's not organized in such strong unions—'

'In other words,' thundered the student, banging the table till the cups rattled in their saucers, 'your father plans to open factories here so that he can exploit our people more than he can exploit yours!'

'Anton Ilyitch!' Madame's eyes blazed as fiercely as

16

his own. 'I must ask you to behave courteously or leave the room!'

'Then I will leave the room!' And muttering angrily in his own language Anton rushed out.

'I apologize for him,' said Madame, refilling the teapot from the samovar tap.

'It's quite like home,' said the Honourable Rosalind with a grin. 'Mummy's friends are rather excitable too.'

The party soon broke up after that. She had to be at the hospital early the next morning, and Sonya, only at home from the Imperial Ballet School because she had been ill, was not supposed to stay up late. Dave himself felt ready for bed.

Madame took him up to his room on the upper floor. It was simple and rather severe, with one weak light-bulb dangling high above the iron bedstead and a jug of hot water standing in the wash-bowl. When she had left him, he pulled aside the curtains but could see only the fog. The windows were double and sealed with putty, as if they were not to be opened until the spring. This, he later discovered, was precisely the idea.

The old maid-servant had set his bags in the middle of the floor. He unpacked hurriedly. Where had he stowed those clean pyjamas? It was then that he came across the package again, the package he had to deliver to Zubova Street. He stood there, weighing it in his hand, wondering once more what was in it.

There was no writing on the brown paper. The girl in Stockholm had gently restrained him from copying down the address. You can carry it in your head, easily, she had insisted.

A birthday present for her grandmother, her dear *babushka* . . . So much safer to have it delivered by hand ... The posts were so untrustworthy with the war and everything ... and once these Customs officials started opening parcels, how could you be sure your harmless little gifts wouldn't be stolen or damaged?

The incident had seemed natural and innocent enough in Stockholm. Now, somehow, in the atmosphere of Russia, he wasn't quite sure.

As he stood there, he heard stealthy footsteps outside the bedroom door. He listened tensely. Then came the gentlest of taps on the panel, twice repeated.

He thrust the package into a drawer. Something impelled him to cover it with clothes before, as the taps came again slightly louder, he called back guardedly:

'Who's there?'

CHAPTER THREE

'For Babushka's Birthday'

A voice behind the panel almost hissed the answer:

'It is I – Anton Ilyitch! Please, I cannot sleep until I have apologized!'

Dave opened the door. The student blundered in, all the clumsier because he was trying to move quietly. He kicked the open suitcase on the floor and nearly fell.

'There's nothing to apologize for,' said Dave.

'But there is, my friend! At our first meeting I insult your father.'

Anton looked quite distraught. He stood there swaying, his hands gesticulating. His hair was wilder than ever, and his tie, which had been askew before, had slipped halfway round to his ear. Dave wanted to laugh but struggled to control himself.

'Aw,' he said, 'my Dad's pretty tough. I guess he wouldn't feel an insult across four thousand miles.'

'But I must explain—'

'Sit down, then.'

Dave didn't want to prolong the conversation far into the night, but he felt that Anton would be safer if he sat still. Anton promptly dropped on to the edge of the bed, which groaned in protest.

'I meant nothing personal,' said the young Russian earnestly. 'It is the system—'

'Sure.'

Anton went on for the next ten minutes about capital-ism, socialism, and several other -isms that Dave had never heard of. It was difficult to follow, because Anton's English grew odder and odder as his excitement rose, and it was British English at that, unfamiliar to a New York ear.

Dave tried to soothe him by interjecting 'Sure . . . sure . . . I understand,' though he was not at all sure and understood very little. But it seemed to do the trick, because suddenly Anton leapt to his feet again with a mighty twangle of thankful bed-springs and seized Dave's hand in a painful grip.

'It is good!' he cried joyfully. 'We shall be friends then. And to show it, if there is something I can do to help you—?' He waited hopefully. He was, Dave decided, rather like a nice dog. A huge, well-meaning, clumsy dog.

All Dave really wanted was to get some sleep. But to say so would have been like kicking the dog. So, on an impulse which he regretted a moment later, he said:

'There *is* one thing. I've got to find an address tomorrow – Zubova Street, number twenty-three, apartment five—'

'Zubova Street?' Anton's sallow face lit up. It was as though the dog had been promised a walk – which in a sense he had. 'I know Zubova Street. After my morning classes I will take you.'

He insisted on wringing Dave's hand again. Then he opened the door a crack and listened. Someone else was moving about. 'I do not wish to meet any of the others tonight,' Anton explained in a whisper. 'I made a fool of myself downstairs. Tomorrow I apologize to Madame. But not now.' He waited. They heard a door close softly in the distance. Anton departed with the stealthy grace of a rhinoceros.

Dave undressed swiftly, hoping that the fog would have cleared by the morning. If it was possible to get lost on the way to Zubova Street, and maybe fall into one of those canals, Anton could be relied upon to do it.

Dave need not have worried. The fog vanished overnight. The morning was crisp and clear.

He slept heavily and rose late, but in St Petersburg, by November, so did the sun. Peering through the window, he saw a narrow strip of blue sky overhead and sparkling blue water at the end of the street.

On the floor below, the big living-room seemed bigger than ever in its morning emptiness. Anton was at the University, Linda Lowdham at the hospital, Sonya standing in line at the butcher's, Miss Upton toddling on her regular constitutional to the Alexander Gardens, Mr Zorin about his business, whatever that was ... Mr Zorin called himself an 'agent'. He was not a man to talk much, preferring to listen, beaming benevolently through his oval spectacles and a pungent cloud of pipe-smoke. As he never referred to the line of goods for which he held the agency, Linda Lowdham used to say it was probably something faintly embarrassing, like plumber's fittings. In which case she jolly well hoped his trade would prosper, because the Russians needed all the modern conveniences they could get.

Madame Mitrova set down Dave's breakfast tray at one end of the table.

'You have slept well, David Davidovitch? I am so glad. Yasha is waiting for your passport – Yasha is the *dvornik*. He must take it to the police. They will give you a permit of residence. Only then can I obtain ration cards for your food.'

He handed over his passport. Then she came back and talked while he drank his pale amber tea and ate the coarse greyish bread with its film of butter. His father, he thought to himself, had wanted him to learn the hard way. Dad should be satisfied if he could see him now.

'Anton has spoken to me,' said Madame with a smile. 'I hope you will be good friends.'

'Sure.'

'For Anton some allowances must be made. His two brothers have been killed on the Austrian front. He has no father. For that reason only he is not called into the army himself. When a widow has only one son, he is not called.'

'Gee, that's tough . . .'

'And, as you see, Anton has much temperament. In the theatre that is of great value. In ordinary life,' Madame added with a chuckle, 'I am not quite so certain.'

'Aw, he seems all right. He's going –' Dave hesitated – 'he's going to show me round a bit, when he's through with his classes.'

'That will be good.'

Anton would not be back until midday, when, it seemed, a sort of cold snack would be served called 'the second breakfast'. Dave was impatient to get out, after so many days cooped up in ships and trains, so he told Madame he would take a walk round the block on his own. He promised not to get lost or to be late.

'You will hear the cannon shoot from the Fortress at twelve o'clock,' she said. 'Everyone in Peters goes by that. We use it to check our clocks.'

He noted that they all spoke of 'St Petersburg' or 'Peters' for short, and seldom remembered to give the city its new name of 'Petrograd'. It had been changed last year, because

'Petersburg' sounded too German, but many people could not get used to the alteration.

St Petersburg or Petrograd – whatever you called the place, it had a heart-catching beauty as it lay there that morning, spread out beneath the autumn sun.

He walked beside the Fontanka Canal until he came to the pink granite embankment overlooking the Neva. The river here was immensely wide, cold, blue, twinkling like a billion diamonds. Long bridges spanned it. That grim mass on the far side must be the Fortress of St Peter and St Paul, where they fired the noonday gun. Yet, so broad was the intervening stretch of water, the ramparts looked no height at all. Only one thing really stood up against the sky, a golden spire, slender as some giant needle, rising from the heart of the citadel.

He remembered that all Petersburg lay flat upon the water, on drained marshes and islets level with the river and the sea. He looked at the plan in his guidebook, then glanced up at the gulls, weaving shrill circles overhead. What a view *they* must have, not that, being gulls, they would appreciate it! From above, the city must look like a cluster of immense water-lilies, each island a blossom of pink and white and yellow stucco walls, with green copper roofs and domes, and interlacing channels of blue water between. He wished he could see it himself from the basket of a balloon or from a flying machine.

He turned and walked briskly along the embankment. Despite the sun the air was sharp. It was, after all, November now. At least, it was back home. Here, Madame had explained, it was still late October. The Russians just had to be different. Not satisfied with an odd alphabet of their own, they kept to an antiquated calendar, lagging thirteen days behind the West.

Soldiers were drilling on a vast square that extended back from the river. They wore long greatcoats and carried their bayonets fixed on their rifles all the time. One company was singing as it marched off the parade-ground. He thought the men sang marvellously, like a trained choir.

Splendid palaces rose in front, their long façades overlooking the Neva on one side and more great empty spaces on the other. He could see more columns of marching infantry. Little wooden men they looked in the distance, across these deserts of paving-stones, dwarfed by the buildings, by triumphal arches and statues . . . It was easy now to believe that St Petersburg was the capital of an empire.

He regained the Pension Yalta just as the midday cannon boomed from the fortress and set the gulls screaming.

Yasha, the janitor, poked his head out of a gloomy doorway at the foot of the stairs, the entrance to his den. He touched the peak of his cap.

'*Passport*,' he murmured. '*Khorosho*.'

Dave knew that the second word meant 'all right'. 'Fine,' he said. '*Spasibo*!' Yasha waited and smiled. Dave had to give him a dollar, because he had not changed any money yet. Yasha looked quite happy about that.

Zubova Street was in the industrial district, on the Viborg Side, said Anton as they set out together after lunch, so it was not likely to be shown on Dave's tourist map. They could take a tram to the Finland Station.

Dave explained about the parcel.

'It was this Russian girl, you see. It was in the hotel when I stopped by in Stockholm.'

'What was her name?'

'Oh, we never got to names.' Dave felt himself going a little pink. 'Don't get me wrong – we didn't talk more than a couple of minutes. Standing by the elevator. She just smiles and says, "You are American? You are on your way to St Petersburg?" Then she says, "You do something for me? I have an old grandmother – it will be her birthday – I want to send her a present, but I do not trust the mail in war-time." I couldn't very well say no, could I?'

'She was beautiful, this girl?'

'I'll say she was. A bit like Sonya. Older though.'

'I wonder what is in this parcel?'

'It feels like books or papers. Maybe the old lady is a reader.'

'Perhaps.' Anton sounded thoughtful. 'Her name also you do not know?'

'No. It's the darnedest thing. I'm just to ring the bell and hand it in, and say "for Babushka's birthday". Does it sound right?' he added anxiously, repeating the phrase in Russian.

'The pronunciation sounds right,' said Anton with a laugh. 'Otherwise, as you say in English, it sounds a little odd.' They had reached the Nevsky. A street-car was approaching. 'It would be better,' he murmured, 'if we did not discuss this matter in the tram.'

'Say, I hope there's nothing crooked about it? She seemed a real nice girl.'

'I am sure she was!'

'And it was nice of her to trust a perfect stranger—'

'And you, too, *you* trusted a perfect stranger! But I think I should have done the same.'

Dave had no chance to reply to that. They crammed themselves into the crowded street-car and went jangling down the broad avenue of the Nevsky Prospect. Hugging the package under one arm, he reflected that he would be extremely thankful to be rid of it.

They must be going back the way he had come last night, over the long Alexander Bridge. And last night's feeling was also coming back, a sense of strangeness and indefinable menace. The beauty of the morning was left behind. The Viborg Side was grey and forbidding. Factory chimneys replaced the gilded spires. Tenements loomed instead of palaces.

They left the street-car at the Finland Station and trudged north. Anton said no more about their errand and Dave did not like to re-open the subject himself. Surely it must be all right, he thought, or Anton would be showing more concern? Anyhow, he had got to deliver the parcel. Whatever misgivings he might have, he couldn't throw it into the river.

They were in the real working-class quarter now. Anton pointed out gloomy, barrack-like buildings adjoining mills and workshops. Here, he said, many of the workers lived in dormitories and cubicles, sometimes two or three famil-ies sharing one small room. Even these conditions might be better than the unspeakable accommodation in the slummier tenements.

'One day I show you,' Anton promised, 'but you will need a strong stomach! I prefer a pig-sty in the country.'

Dave listened to his non-stop commentary about the sufferings of the poor. His father would have dismissed Anton as a typical College intellectual, with high ideals maybe, but no horse sense. But what he said was interest-ing, all that stuff about wages and working hours and living conditions – things a business man had to know too, things Dad had told him to notice. Dave resolved to check up later and see if Anton had got his facts straight.

His own eyes and nose warned him that life was tough for folks living on the Viborg Side.

Zubova Street was a cut above the neighbouring slums. It was cobbled, with a paved sidewalk. There were some small shops and on one corner a *traktir*, or workmen's tea-bar. A little further down, and on the opposite side of the street, they found the house they wanted, a three-storey building, one of the better ones, with lace curtains at the windows and pot-plants.

They stepped through the open doorway. There was no sign of a *dvornik*, but a woman was just coming out of a ground-floor apartment with a child, and she stared at them, asking something in a helpful tone.

There was a brief conversation that Dave could not understand, though he recognized the number 'five'. The woman kept shaking her head, and the child shook its head in agreement. Finally the woman shrugged her shoulders a little huffily, and jerked the child's hand, and the pair set off down the street.

Anton looked puzzled, but he started up the stairs with Dave at his heels.

'She says,' he explained, 'that there is no old woman living at Number Five.'

'But—'

'We shall ask. Neighbours do not know everything – though they think they do!'

There were two apartment doors, left and right, at each landing. They were a little breathless when they reached Number Five. Anton rang the bell.

'Do you think—' Dave began.

'Always I think,' said Anton with a grin. 'They tell me I think more than is good.'

The door looked very blank. But when he rang again,

it opened with startling suddenness. Only about twelve inches, however. Wide enough to reveal a pale, rather tense-looking face. It belonged to a smallish, middle-aged man. Dave would have guessed Jewish. He had seen the type often at home. New York had lots of Russian and Polish Jews who'd emigrated because they had such a bad time of it under the government of the Tsar.

Again he could grasp only an odd word or two of the dialogue. But when Anton mentioned Stockholm the man's face lit up with a new interest, and at the word '*babushka*' his guarded expression melted into a warm friendliness. Even so, though he opened the door wider, he made no gesture to invite them in. He almost snatched the parcel from Dave's extended hands, stammered voluble thanks, bowed, smiled – and shut the door.

Dave followed Anton downstairs again feeling slightly piqued. He'd been thanked . . . he hadn't expected a lot of fuss . . . but he'd have liked a glimpse of the old grand-mother, a word or two about what the girl was doing in Sweden . . .

Anton would have interpreted. As it was, he had the irritating sensation of unfinished business, of a puzzle left unsolved.

'Well, that's that,' he said as they reached the side-walk again.

But it wasn't. They had taken only a few paces when a car came round the corner and stopped. Two hefty men in soft hats and greenish overcoats jumped out of the back seats. Without a moment's hesitation they marched across to the doorway from which the boys had just emerged.

'We had better get out of here,' muttered Anton hoarsely. 'It is the Ochrana – the Secret Police.'

CHAPTER FOUR

Was it Coincidence?

Anton did not quicken his pace. 'We must walk naturally,' he warned Dave. 'Do not look back.' Suddenly he changed direction. 'A glass of tea, I think.'

He steered Dave across the cobbled road to the *traktir*. Inside, a soldier and a couple of steel-workers were munching slices of rye bread with rings of cold sausage. Anton pushed Dave on to a bench by the window, went to the counter, and fetched two glasses of steaming tea. He spilt some as he collided with one of the workmen, who cursed him ferociously and then turned back to his companions.

'This is safe enough,' Anton grunted as he joined Dave on the bench.

'Safe—?'

'The tea.'

'Oh.'

'Never drink water in Petersburg unless it has been boiled.'

'I see. When you said "safe", I thought you meant—'

'That also, yes. I think we are all right in here.' Anton pulled off his peaked University cap and hid it inside his waistcoat.

Dave was still bemused by the suddenness with which things had happened in the last five minutes. He had grasped that something fishy was going on inside the house they had just left and he could understand Anton's anxiety not to get mixed up in it.

'But why didn't we carry on walking?' he whispered.

'Because I saw another car – just in time! You did not notice it? It stopped at the end of the street. It was more of the – the same gentlemen.' Anton glanced round warily, but the other customers were arguing loudly and could not possibly have been listening, even if any of them had understood English, which was extremely unlikely. 'I thought,' Anton continued, 'they might be throwing a cordon round the area. They cannot question every one in all the houses. But they can stop those who pass through the cordon. So, for the moment, it is better – as you say – to lie low.'

'But – we've done nothing!'

Anton shrugged his shoulders contemptuously. 'In this country it is not necessary to do anything. However, did we not deliver a package? From abroad?'

'Holy smoke! Is that against the law?'

'Possibly.'

'Why did you let me?'

'I despise the law!' Anton spoke with tremendous intensity. Aware of Dave's surprise he went on: 'It is hard for you to understand. Your laws you make yourselves. Ours are imposed upon us. A man who believes in liberty cannot feel bound by them.'

Dave saw his point. But he was in no mood to listen to one of the student's long political speeches. Nervously he peered out through the dusty window of the *traktir*, thankful for the tall plant which screened his face from passers-by.

The car was still drawn up by the kerb opposite. The driver was standing beside it. A small crowd had gathered, watching from a safe distance, and there were faces at the windows up and down the street.

'Looks like the police all right. It was real smart of you to spot them straight off like that.'

'It is easy. You can always tell them. They wear those pea-green overcoats. And whatever the weather they have their galoshes!' Anton laughed sardonically. 'I suppose in their work they must be prepared for everything.'

He seemed to be taking the affair very lightly, thought Dave. But it wasn't so funny. Not so funny at all. Lowering his voice still more, he inquired:

'What would happen to *us*? I mean, if—'

'To you, nothing much. You show them your American passport—'

'I haven't got it! The janitor took it!'

'Of course! Then there would be delay while they checked – they might hold you till tomorrow – they can be very slow, very inefficient—'

Dave went cold inside. He saw himself spending a night in the cells. He tried to imitate Anton's devil-may-care attitude but it wasn't easy.

'That all?' he said.

'Yes, I think so. Except—'

'Except what?'

'There might be trouble about your residential permit.'

'You mean – they might sling me out? Ship me back to the States?' Cold before, Dave now froze with horror. He could imagine what his father would say.

'Do not worry. Behave calmly.'

Anton pulled out some cigarettes. They seemed to consist mainly of hollow paper tubes with a small quantity of rank tobacco packed into one end. He offered them to Dave, who refused, then lit one himself.

'It's all very well for you,' Dave grumbled. '*You* can't be expelled.'

'Oh yes, my friend. From the University. From the city also. It has happened to several friends of mine. And it is sufficiently serious. A black mark against you for the rest of your life.'

'I'm sorry. Then it could be worse for you.'

'I tell you, do not worry. Ah, something is happening yonder!'

There was a stir among the spectators down the street. The police driver took a step forward, bracing himself for action. Dave glanced hastily at the other customers in the *traktir*. It was better that they should remain unaware of the drama outside, or they might start noticing the boys and asking questions. Luckily they still seemed to be absorbed in their own affairs.

'Look!' Anton breathed the word softly.

The men in green overcoats were bringing somebody out of Number Twenty-three. It was the little Jew from the upstairs apartment. He was handcuffed. One of the men shoved him into the back of the car and climbed in.

'Poor devil!' murmured Anton.

The second policeman was carrying the parcel. It had been untied and only loosely wrapped up again. One flap of brown paper wavered in the breeze, and, as he crossed the side-walk, there was a scattering of white handbills. They drifted across the pavement like autumn leaves. The policeman stooped, gathering them up awkwardly with one hand, stuffing them crumpled into his overcoat pocket, while with the other hand he pressed the parcel to his side.

There was a ripple of comment from the bystanders, low but hostile.

'Seems the cops haven't a lot of friends in this area,' Dave commented.

'Cops?' Anton sounded puzzled. His English studies had left him stronger on Shakespeare than on slang.

'Skip it.'

'Skip—?'

It would have been funny at any other time. Just now Dave was in no mood to give a language lesson. It was too grim, seeing that little Jewish guy hustled into the car. It could have been Anton and himself. And they weren't out of the wood yet.

The policeman thrust the parcel into the empty seat in front and then walked towards the crowd, pulling out a notebook. If it had been a revolver it could not have dispersed them more effectively. Zubova Street did not wish to be involved with the Secret Police. The bystanders melted away.

'Darn it!' Dave pressed his nose against the window. 'She would turn up!'

'Who?'

'That woman from downstairs!'

The woman with the child had come down the street at the worst possible moment. They watched the policeman accost her. The little girl raised her free hand excitedly and began to babble something. The policeman bent at the knees, listening and encouraging her. After that, obviously, the mother had to talk, whether she had meant to or not, and the policeman straightened up to write something in his notebook. Then he opened the car door again and they all peered in, not at the prisoner in the back but at the parcel on the seat beside the driver. Mother and child wagged their heads emphatically. The policeman scribbled.

'Aw, heck!' Dave groaned. 'They're identifying the parcel. They're describing *us*.'

He gave himself up for lost. He could see the whole horrible future unrolling before him like a motion picture, from a tight-lipped Mr Hayes seeing him off again at the Finland Station to a tight-lipped Mr Hopkins bounding up the gang-plank to greet him (if not exactly welcome him) in New York.

'It will be all right,' said Anton. 'You did not open your mouth: she can say only that you had foreign clothes. As for me, there are thousands of students in caps like mine. And ninety per cent of them wish to overthrow the Government. So where are the authorities to look?'

'They might start by looking here!'

'No, no. They will assume that we are now miles away.'

'I hope you're right.'

'I am. See.'

The car door slammed. The driver cranked up the engine and got in. The car turned and sped away. The mother and child gaped after it, then the mother seized the child and hurried her into the house. She looked as if she did not want to meet any of the neighbours just then.

Anton slid along the bench and stood up, pulling out a handful of small coins. 'While I pay, look out of the doorway – but casually, not like a villain in a play! See if the other car is still at the end of the street.'

'Okay.'

Dave moved to the door and stuck his nose out into the welcome fresh air as if to inspect the weather. There was no sign of a car in either direction or of any watchful figure. It would be dark soon. The sunset was already a coppery blur at the end of the street, though it was only three o'clock.

He turned and caught Anton's eye reassuringly. The student followed him out.

'Go on in front, and wait round the corner, in the main boulevard.'

'But—'

'Go. I will not be a moment. They are looking for two together – if they are looking at all.'

Dave saw the point. He went without further argument. It seemed a good idea to cross at once to the other side of the street, the same side as Number Twenty-three. Then, if the woman on the ground floor or her tiresome child happened to look out of the window, he would be more quickly hidden from their view.

He had the impression – though he dared not turn his head – that Anton had also crossed the road, but slanting the other way, on a line that would take him straight to the house. He hoped that Anton knew what he was doing. Surely he wasn't crazy enough to go back there? And why, for goodness sake?

But Anton had promised that he would not be a moment, and he kept his word. He rejoined Dave in the busy main thoroughfare, where the crowded sidewalks offered a welcome sense of concealment.

'I have one of the leaflets that fell,' he announced triumphantly. 'One that the policeman missed.'

'So that's why you went back? Gee, you sure do take chances.'

'Those who are afraid of bears should not go into the woods.'

'What's the leaflet about?'

'I am not such a fool that I stand and read such things in a public place! I shall show it to you when we get home. But in my room. Not a word to anyone.'

They went back by another way, crossing a branch of the river called the Great Nevka, past the looming blackness of St Peter and St Paul with its rapier spire stabbing the yellow sky, and over the Trinity Bridge to the now-familiar embankment of the Neva. The gas street-lamps were being lit but the city was dim. Anton explained that the electricity was cut off until six o'clock.

So, when they reached his bedroom next to Dave's, they had to examine the leaflet by candle-light. It was printed in heavy black type. Dave could spell out a few of the short, familiar words and others that were almost the same as English. There was no missing one word: *'Revolution'*.

Anton gabbled a rough translation in a discreet undertone. There was something highly uncomplimentary about the Tsar: he was referred to as 'the anointed butcher'. There was something about some adviser of his named Rasputin, 'that evil spirit that is dragging our country down into ruin'. There was an appeal to the people to rise up in their millions and sweep away the old order.

'Say, who prints this stuff?' Dave asked.

'Prints?' Anton shrugged. 'In Russia it is illegal, because of the censorship. There are, of course, secret printing presses. But sometimes the work is done abroad and smuggled in.'

'I mean – publishes it. Hands it out.'

'Ah – I see! This leaflet is the work of a small group – we have many groups and parties, too many to remember them all. This is not a good group,' said Anton loftily. 'It is – what do you say? – amateurish. Look at their methods! Small parcels of leaflets, smuggled in by helpful strangers! What can they achieve? They are like children playing a game. It is not a game.'

'I guess not,' said Dave with feeling. 'Anyway, it's given

me an exciting afternoon. I don't want to go through all that again.'

'It was very bad luck – the police raiding the house just as we were coming away.'

'Luck?' Dave had a sudden thought and it was not at all a pleasant one. Because, if he was right, they might still be in danger of trouble. 'Suppose,' he went on, 'it was something more than a nasty coincidence?'

'What do you mean?'

'Suppose the police timed their raid because they knew the leaflets were going to be delivered today and they'd be sure of finding the evidence they wanted? It was just too neat to be natural. And in that case – *who tipped them off*?'

CHAPTER FIVE

Sonya

Anton stared, his eyes wide in the candle-light.

'You think that possible? But who could know? To whom had you spoken of this besides me?'

'No one,' said Dave without hesitation. And he added quickly: 'Obviously it wasn't *you* – any more than me. Could some one have heard us last night when we were talking in my room?'

'It is possible. But who would do such a thing?'

'Isn't the *dvornik* a sort of police informer?'

'Oh, yes. But he lives in the basement. He has no access to the Pension.'

'Not officially. But if it was back home in the States – if you can imagine such a thing – a guy in his position would somehow get hold of a key. You bet.'

'Yasha may have such a key. But he would never dare to use it when the apartment was full of people. It was not late. He might have met Madame or any one.'

Dave saw the force of that. 'I give up,' he said. 'Unless he works with the old servant—'

'Anya? Anya would not spy. She is good. She quarrels all the time with Yasha. And you forget – Anya understands no English. What purpose to listen at your door?'

'No. That wasn't very bright of me. Come to that, Yasha doesn't seem to know English either.'

'Ah! I wonder . . . It is possible that Yasha knows more than he reveals. It would be an advantage, in his position, to conceal his knowledge. But where would he acquire such knowledge? He has no education. In any case, we have excluded him. It is not possible he was in the apartment.'

'I still have a hunch it was more than coincidence, the way those cops arrived in Zubova Street. There'd been a leak somewhere.'

'A leak? Ah, I understand, a leak of information! Yes – but another thing you forget, my friend. The leak could have been in Sweden. If you have mentioned that address to no one but myself, the leak *must* have been in Sweden.'

'Could that happen?'

'Why not? The Ochrana has long arms – it reaches everywhere. It tries to plant its agents in every revolution-ary organization to find out their plans. Not only at home in Russia, but wherever there is a group of exiles abroad – in Paris, London, Switzerland, and no doubt Stockholm. You must not worry, David Davidovitch. I think it was nothing to do with you or with this house. Someone was spying on that girl in the hotel. Then that person sent a telegram to Ochrana headquarters here.'

The Ochrana, Anton explained, was a separate wing of the police organization, concerned only with political security. It had fingerprints and dossiers of everyone sus-pected of revolutionary activity. People said that it pos-sessed the most complete library of subversive books and pamphlets in the world. It employed hundreds of agents in Petersburg, Moscow and the other main cities, besides such part-time informers as the *dvorniks*. The man who sold you your newspaper or drove your taxi might be a trained member of the Ochrana. There was a wardrobe of uniforms and disguises, it was rumoured, that would not have disgraced the Imperial Opera House.

'They work patiently,' said Anton. 'They like to find out everything about a particular organization, collect all the evidence and every name, and then spring the trap! But they can hold a suspect only for fifteen days without making a charge—'

'Fifteen days!' Dave exclaimed. 'They couldn't do that in the States. Say, you seem to know a heck of a lot about all this!'

'There is much talk of these things among the students.'

'I guess you had your own ideas about that parcel all along?'

Anton grinned. 'I cannot lie to you.'

'And you took me along to Zubova Street, knowing all the time—'

'I knew nothing for certain,' Anton protested. 'And I can assure you, I had no idea that there would be a police raid. I would not have led you into such danger. I was merely curious, myself—'

'You're not mixed up with these people?' Dave demanded suspiciously, pointing to the words at the bottom of the leaflet.

'No. I have heard of them.'

'But you agree with them?'

Anton's head went up and his eyes challenged Dave's. 'In general terms, of course. Every intelligent person in Russia knows that revolution will come – must come. We disagree only on methods.'

Dave realized why Mr Hayes had said, last night, that the kids in Russia were crazy about politics. He recalled, too, the diplomat's warning to watch his step. After what had happened in the first twenty-four hours he began to see the sense in that advice.

An unpleasant thought occurred to him. He swung round, seized the door-knob, and opened the door so abruptly that the candle-flame streamed sideways and almost went out. To his relief there was no one on the landing.

Anton gave an appreciative chuckle. 'You will make a good conspirator,' he whispered.

'Aw, shut up, will you?' Dave was irritated by his own nervousness. 'It's not what I came to this country for. I've got my own worries. I'm keeping out of yours.'

For his first few days in St Petersburg Dave lived in a state of suspense, keyed up to meet trouble. When the door-bell rang he braced himself for unwelcome visitors in green overcoats and galoshes. When he saw Yasha downstairs, peeking from his shadowy cubbyhole to see who was coming in or going out, he felt a quite illogical spasm of guilt and hurried past as though he really had something to hide.

Gradually, though, the feeling wore off. Nothing unpleasant occurred. His residential permit came through and Madame obtained his ration cards. He received his first mail from home. He had to collect it from the American Embassy. It was quicker and safer than the ordinary service.

During the daytime he built up a regular routine. After breakfast, while his brain was fresh, he put in a steady hour or two at Russian. He learnt grammar and word-lists, hammered away at simple passages with a dictionary, tried out his pronunciation on Madame, Sonya, even Anya, anyone who strayed into the living-room while he was at work.

When he had done as much as he could stand, he muffled himself up in coat and scarf and a round fur hat he had bought and was secretly proud of (it looked as though he were going out to shoot wolves or grizzlies or something) and spent the few remaining hours of daylight exploring the city. Sometimes Anton went with him, occasionally Linda if she had time off from the hospital. Most often it was Sonya, who was supposed to take fresh air and exercise before going back into school.

With Sonya he could really *see* St Petersburg.

With Anton he might cover miles, but it was talk, talk, talk – Anton forever going on about the dreadful state of Russia and the wickedness of Rasputin, a weird kind of holy man from the depths of Siberia (and not so holy at that, by all accounts) who dominated the Empress and so pretty well dominated the Emperor too. All very interesting at first, but Anton's non-stop indignation could be wearisome.

Linda liked talking too. With her it was gossip from the hospital and funny stories about her family. Her bright chatter came between him and the Russia he wanted to see.

Sonya was different. She was silent and serene. She would answer his questions – if she knew the answer. But often she did not. She was curiously remote from everyday life. She lived in the narrow, brilliant, absorbing world of the Imperial Ballet School. She was one of the senior girls, nearing the end of her seven-year course.

Together they strolled for hours. Sonya would throw out an arm in a graceful gesture, point a gloved finger at something worth noticing, and murmur the absolute minimum – identifying a building or a statue or just com-

menting on a leafless tree, a light-effect upon the water . . .
'Beautiful, yes?' Sometimes she said nothing at all, just
pressed his arm or caught his eye if they were standing
still, so that he looked in the right direction and did not
miss whatever it was.

'Peter the Great,' she would murmur.

And there, in the centre of the enormous square, backed
by St Isaac's Cathedral with its glittering gilded dome,
would be this staggering statue of the city's founder, his
charger rearing up on its hindlegs with a red granite crag
for pedestal, as though about to plunge forward the next
moment into the cannon-smoke.

'Anton's university . . .' And across the river on Vassily
Island stretched the long façade, the walls a soft warm
red, cheerful in the nipping air.

'The Smolny Convent . . .' And he saw a cluster of
baroque buildings, with shallow domes, softly blue, the
colour of camp-fire smoke, faintly picked out in old gold.

And another afternoon, 'My school,' she whispered. It
had a long classical frontage, with pairs of columns divid-
ing the tall windows, and carved garlands and wreaths
of stonework, very elegant, and the double-headed eagle of
the Tsars over the portico. 'We are not supposed to look
out of those windows,' she told him with a laugh. 'The
glass is – how do you say?'

'Frosted? So's you can't see through?'

'Yes, frosted. All but the top panes. Of course the girls
climb up, so that they can look down into the street. But
we have to be very gymnastic! We must not fall and break
our legs. Even a twisted ankle is a tragedy.'

He could believe that – if the other pupils were as keen
as she was. He knew how her own convalescence irked
her. She had had some sort of fever, with a lingering

infection, and the director of the Ballet School had sent her home until the doctor should pronounce her clear.

It was tough on Sonya. For himself, he could not complain. She was good to go around with.

After dinner the long evenings were mostly spent all together in the living-room, with ten o'clock tea round the samovar before bed.

Often there was music. Anton would forget politics and strum on his balalaika, while the other Russians joined him in one of their peasant songs. Sonya would go to the piano and play Chopin or Tchaikovsky. Linda, called on to take her turn, would protest that she could play nothing but ragtime – which she did, gaily and noisily, until a disapproving Miss Upton begged her to cease. Miss Upton hated ragtime and thought Tchaikovsky unhealthy because he was too emotional. She would enthrone herself on the piano stool and tinkle out tunes from the Sullivan operas or (if it was Sunday) from *Hymns Ancient and Modern*.

Miss Upton spent much of the evening playing ludo by herself, shaking the dice and moving the counters for her three invisible opponents. Once, on a kind impulse, Dave offered to take part. She looked up at him and agreed rather grudgingly.

'You may move Fedor's counters if you like.'

'Fedor? Er – what colour?'

'The green, of course. Fedor always chose green.'

Later in the evening Dave whispered to Linda: 'Did I do the wrong thing? Who the heck is this Fedor she kept on about? And Mikhail and "dear little Alexandrina"?'

'They were the Prince's children in her last place. I don't know what else she taught them, but she taught them ludo! They seem to have played night after night in the palace nursery.'

'Is she dotty or something?'

'Oh, not really. But she lives in the past. Can you blame her? All her happiness was in the past. Bit pathetic, really.'

Dave never offered to play again.

Anton was sometimes out in the evenings on his own affairs. University clubs and meetings, he explained. At other times he would shut himself up in the quiet of his chilly bedroom when he had an essay or a passage of translation to do for his professor.

Mr Zorin was another – small wonder, in view of the music and chatter – who sought refuge in his own room when he had a letter to write. This happened two or three times a week and was faintly mysterious. Mr Zorin would reappear, swathed against the weather outside, clutching an envelope in his gloved paw and announcing that he was just going to the post and would be back in time for the tea. Even when he had a bad cough and it was snowing hard, he would never allow any of the younger ones to do the errand for him. He insisted on braving the raw December night himself. It became a standing joke with the others.

'It is something too important for him to trust us,' said Anton. 'Perhaps it is business, the orders he has taken.'

'That's it,' said Linda. 'Great long lists of lavatory fittings!'

'No,' said Sonya. 'I think he is in love.' And when they all exploded with laughter at the very idea she went on quietly: 'Has any one ever seen the address on the envelope? No! He takes care we do not. I am sure it is a lady – a lady for whom our poor friend cherishes a hopeless but undying passion.'

'It is certainly hopeless, then,' said Anton. 'Because she never writes back. He never gets any letters at all.'

'I am not surprised,' Madame rebuked him, 'when you young scamps gossip about him so shamelessly. No doubt he has his private letters sent to his place of business, wherever that is. And let me tell you, it is not impossible – and it is not funny – if an older person falls in love. You think everything in the world is for you, and for you only. No more gossip, now!' But her twinkling eyes belied her stern tone. 'I shall pour the tea. At any moment Josef Andreievitch will be back.'

Dave also wrote letters. His mother wanted to know if Madame was looking after him properly, if he was getting enough to eat, and if he had made any nice friends. To his father, though, he had to send more serious reports.

'*I am still trying to get the hang of the way this country is run,*' he wrote. '*They have nothing really like our Congress or the British Parliament. They do elect something called the Duma, but it doesn't meet very often and it hasn't much power, and Anton (the student I told you about, who rooms here) says it's nothing but a talking-shop. The Tsar has absolute power, the way kings and emperors did back in history, and what he says goes. But by all accounts he's a good-natured weak-willed guy, who mostly does what his wife tells him. Right now he's away with his armies – trying to run the war himself, personally, I ask you! – so the Tsarina has even more control over everything else. They say she listens too much to some peasant preacher or holy man, called Rasputin, and right now he is more the genuine ruler of Russia than either of them. One way and another, this place seems to be in a queer state. There's no efficiency. Linda hears awful things from the wounded who come in to her hospital. Soldiers without boots, no shells for the guns, regiments with only one rifle for every three men. And don't imagine they have*' *no labour troubles here – they have strikes same as back home. If you ask me, I would think twice before investing any dollars in Russia, the way things are . . .'*

Dave thought it wiser to say nothing about the secret police, let alone about his own little adventure with them. Even so, he knew it was as well that his letter was going home via the Embassy, and not through the ordinary mails.

CHAPTER SIX

Champagne and Gipsies

Now winter came, the third winter of the great war. The cold blew out of the flat eastern lands and withered Europe. 'I do not recall a worse December,' said Madame Mitrova. The war doubled its harshness.

On the Western Front the interwoven trenches zigzagged from neutral Switzerland to the North Sea. The Germans, French, and British held their ground, grey-faced but determined. Winter, for all its rigòurs, halted the summer's butchery. The big battles faded out. Three-quarters of a million men had been killed or wounded at Verdun, and as many on the Somme.

The Eastern Front was even longer, and much vaguer. The patriotic Miss Upton pinned tiny flags on her old nursery wall-map, Russian, Rumanian, German, Austro-Hungarian, dotting them from the Baltic to the Black Sea, but the distances were so great, the news so scrappy, that she could not keep pace with the situation. 'The papers always say that we are advancing,' she complained, 'yet every time a place is mentioned by name it seems to be further to the east.'

Linda brought heart-rending stories from the hospital, though the cases did not come straight from the front and she knew she was not seeing the full horror. Yet even in those clean, neat wards in the Grand Duke's palace she heard what it was like where the shells were falling.

'They're so brave,' she said, 'but they can't fight the Huns with their bare hands. Even a Russian can't survive in this weather without proper food and equipment. No wonder the troops are deserting in thousands! The war's being shockingly mismanaged at the top.'

For once she wasn't smiling. Her lip quivered and her eyes were hot with furious tears. Her Mom must have looked like that, thought Dave, when she tussled with the London cops and demanded votes for women.

Despite Linda's grim reports, despite the electricity cuts and the shortages of food and fuel and candles, there were moments when he forgot the war and fell captive to the city's spell.

The deep frost came, transforming Petersburg. Overnight the narrow canals froze white and olive green, the Moika Canal and the Caterina, and the Fontanka under their own windows.

Soon the cold tamed the wider waterways. Ice spread like a skin across the Great Neva, the Little Neva, the three channels of the Nevka. The skin joined, thickened, skin no longer but horn. Then it was not horn but burnished steel. The summer pontoon bridge that had stretched from the Winter Palace across to the University had been taken away. Anton and the other students began, daringly, to run across the ice to their lectures, heedless of shouted protests from the policemen. By next day, all danger past, the river was a thoroughfare. Workmen rigged up temporary lighting. The ice was two feet thick. Droshkies could drive on it.

Snow followed, blowing in across the Ural Mountains from Siberia. When it stopped, and the sun came out at noon, it was hard to tell where the land and water met. The mosaic of islands was cemented into one sparkling whiteness. The colours seemed brighter than ever by contrast, the warm red walls of the University, the pink granite embankments, the golds and greens of spire and cupola. Palaces and churches took on an enhanced splendour, their lines picked out in silver by the crusted snow.

Night brought a new magic. The droshkies now sped on runners. Muffled in long overcoats, their waiting drivers swung arms and stamped boots beside street-corner fires, which threw a lambent rosy light on walls and roadway. 'Christmas Cake City!' Linda called it. The street-cars jangling down the Nevsky were touched with romance, as the blue sparks flashed and crackled, turning the trolley-poles to fairy wands.

Dave was glad he had remembered his skates. He could hold his own with Anton and Sonya. Poor Linda fell about all over the place, delirious with laughter, gasping that in England the frost never held long enough for her to master the technique.

'Ah, you should have been here in the old days,' Miss Upton grumbled. 'So many more lights, all colours, so very charming. And the bands! They played waltzes on the ice. The best people were there, such pretty skating costumes, and the officers wore their real uniforms, not these dreadfully drab ones they have now.' She sighed. 'It was so lively, you can't imagine. We kept it up till three in the morning. Yes, even little me! Nothing is the same now. No elegance, no night life—'

'There is plenty of night life,' Anton contradicted her. 'Walk into the Europa Hotel – or the Astoria. Full of fat profiteers and officers who should be at the front, swilling champagne as if it were water!'

'How do you know, young man? Have you seen them?'

'It is common knowledge.'

'Gossip! Propaganda! You talk like an agitator,' said Miss Upton huffily. She revered the Tsar, the aristocracy, the army, the whole imperial system. She would not hear a word against them.

Dave's allowance was moderate. His father was strict but he trusted Dave. So there was a reserve fund for emergencies and reasonable extras.

'Above all,' Mr Hopkins had counselled him, 'I don't want my son to be thought a tightwad. If folks are good to you, find some real nice way to repay them.'

Mindful of this, Dave wanted to treat his three young friends to an evening out. It must be soon, because Sonya was nearly fit and would be going back to school. She was hoping for a tiny part in the public performance of *Swan Lake*. Every day, religiously, she kept up her exercises.

It must be an evening, too, when Linda did not work late at the hospital, and when Anton was not tied up with any of his student activities. It would do Anton good, thought Dave, to have fun for once.

'Where could we go?' he asked.

Anton considered gravely. 'Chaliapin is singing at the Opera – it is hard to get tickets, but—'

Dave made a face. Grand opera was not his idea of a lively evening.

'A play by Chekhov, perhaps?'

Dave groaned. 'Really, Anton! You forget,' he said quickly. 'Linda's Russian isn't so hot. Apart from mine!'

'Of course! I am sorry. Let me see.' Anton frowned, trying to come down to Dave's level. The new Charlie

Chaplin film would not be new to an American – Linda too had probably seen it before leaving England. The Christmas circus would not have opened... Suddenly Anton brightened. 'I have it! The gipsies!'

There were gipsy taverns, he explained, where they could get some kind of supper, even in war-time, and there would be singing and dancing. The gipsies were genuine, their costumes wonderful. The girls would adore it.

'But,' he added with a conspiratorial air, 'we had better tell no one where we are going. Keep that as a surprise. Madame might hesitate... and the Ballet School might not approve.'

'Hey, it's not some sort of low dive?' Dave hesitated between caution and curiosity. 'I mean it's okay we take the girls there?'

'Of course, of course! I shall inquire and choose one that is respectable. I have friends who know these places well.'

So it was arranged. The girls were delighted to accept their invitation to this mysterious outing. Madame pursed her lips and looked canny, but did not press for detailed guarantees. They must not stay out too late, that was her one condition. Sonya was officially on sick-leave. She must be sensible.

'But of course, *babushka*!'

With the thought of *Swan Lake* never far from her mind, Sonya could be relied upon to behave herself. But she was as thrilled as Linda when they reached the street and were let into the secret of the evening's programme.

The gipsies all lived on the Viborg Side at Novaya Derevnaya. It was beyond the islands. Anton said they would need a taxi.

'Not on your life!' said Dave. 'We'll go in one of these droshky things!'

In the end they hired two. Linda went with Anton, laughing and exclaiming that she felt like Father Christmas, while Dave followed with Sonya. As usual she said little, but seemed happy enough, snuggled in her fur coat with a white lamb's-wool hood framing her face. Their breath steamed under the pallid street-lamps. Their cheeks tingled.

It was an unforgettable drive. Snow muted the hoof-beats of the shaggy little horse and the sigh of the gliding runners. There was only the incessant tinkle of small bells, a rare whip-crack, a bass oath from the *izvozchik* as another driver got in his way.

Overhead, the stars were as sharp as cut diamonds. Beneath, the snow was a deep-pile carpet, the Nevka channels so many shining satin ribbons that curled away to the frozen Gulf. Time stood still. Nothing suggested 1916. It could have been 1816, even 1716, the enchanted city fresh from Peter the Great's compulsively creative hands.

Time stood still. But the two droshkies sped on.

Then suddenly, 'Come on, you two!' Linda was calling. 'This is it. We've arrived!' They unwound themselves and clambered out, and Anton paid with the money Dave had given him, and they pressed through a lighted doorway into the heat and noise within.

A wrinkled dame with huge earrings seized their caps and coats. A gipsy youth swaggered in front of them, smiling and glib. They saw the band grouped in the centre of the room. On three sides, raised a few steps, were the tables, looking down over a balustrade. Each table was separated from its neighbour by a trelliswork partition.

The place was not very full as yet, for it was early, but the musicians had already warmed to their work. They looked as colourful as Anton had promised. The men wore

Russian blouses of the brightest, most garish hues, their voluminous trousers stuffed into high top-boots. The women who sang or swirled in the open space, banging and rattling their tambourines, had gaudy shawls and kerchiefs. They glittered with sequins and massive bracelets. Their long skirts spun round the floor like whirlpools.

Dave stared down at them fascinated, the gipsy-girls twirling and posturing, the men scraping their fiddles like furies.

'It is usual to order champagne,' Anton whispered anxiously, as the waiter took their order for supper.

'Sure! You explained. Go right ahead.'

A bottle was brought, and the gipsy's deft brown fingers untwisted the wire fastening, and the cork flew ceilingwards with an impressive pop, and the pale golden wine frothed into their glasses. The waiter bowed solemnly, yet somehow mockingly, as he placed a brimming glass in front of Dave.

'You are supposed to drink it all at once, without pausing,' said Anton. 'It is a custom.'

'Okay.'

Dave seized the glass with some alarm. Until now, his acquaintance with champagne had been limited to a few family weddings. One glass, sipped between nibbles of cake, had been about his limit. To swallow it all at one go was another matter. However, conscious that the eyes of the girls were upon him (and thankful that his father's were not), he raised his glass, tilted his head back, and gulped down the wine.

'Bravo!' cried Sonya, and clapped her hands.

The room grew – or seemed – hotter, the music wilder. Plaintive, gay and passionate by turns, the violins wailed and throbbed, the voices vibrated through the hazy air.

Anton translated the song-titles: 'Black Eyes', 'Once Again', 'Two Guitars', 'I Cannot Forget' . . . and between the singing the dancers gyrated madly, turned, flashed their eyes, snapped their fingers, and waved their tinselled tambourines.

There was one girl Anton specially admired. He said so. But Sonya shook her head with unusual vehemence.

'Never! She has no technique.'

'But what passion!'

'Feeling is necessary. But discipline also. These girls have no training. They are not true artists. They are animals.'

'Ha!' cried Anton. 'There speaks the Imperial Ballet School – through its illustrious ballerina-to-be!'

'Hold your tongue, Anton Ilyitch!' But it was Sonya herself who relapsed, after that outburst, into her more usual silence. Linda caught Dave's eye amusedly. He had never seen Sonya so roused. Nor had he known Anton speak so warmly of a girl. Perhaps in both cases it was the champagne.

The place was filling up now. There were cadets in their brand-new uniforms, chattering noisily and very pleased with themselves. There were middle-aged business men, gesticulating with long cigars, and ladies in evening dress, scented and jewelled. The corks were popping on all sides.

Linda teased Anton. 'Don't look so glum!'

'Glum? Ah – it angers me to see all this.'

'Oh, come on, enjoy yourself!'

Anton turned to Dave apologetically. 'Do not misunderstand, please. For us, for this one evening, for the experience, this is interesting. But every night! Like these people!' He rolled his eyes in disgust. 'Where do they get the money? This is a city of corruption. Those fat men with their fat cigars – they are speculators.'

'Speculators?'

'They buy up everything, they hoard it, then they sell at high prices. I heard of one – he bought coffee in Vladivostok for seventy roubles the pood and sells it here in Peters at four hundred. It is so with everything. We are supposed to be equal in this war, to have our rations, rich and poor alike. But the rich and poor are *not* alike! Always the rich get round the regulations, the officials are bribed, the speculators make fortunes while, the masses starve—'

'Come off it, Anton,' Linda interrupted. 'No politics tonight!'

A fortune-teller was coming round the tables. She was ancient and bent, slow-moving but with a strange primitive majesty. She came into the young people's box and fixed them with her eyes, glittering serpentine eyes set in the skinny folds of her sunken face. The girls begged her to tell their fortunes. She seized Linda's pink scrubbed nurse's hand, turned it over and peered into the palm.

Sonya translated, for Anton sat aloof and disapproving. 'You are to make a long journey across water . . .'

'That is easy,' snorted Anton. 'It is obvious that Linda is English – so how else can she ever go home?'

When it was Sonya's turn it was hard to persuade her to translate her own fortune. She giggled excitedly and went pink. 'I am soon to attract the attention of a great personage,' she finally confessed.

'Fine,' said Dave. 'You'll marry a Grand Duke or something.'

'That's not what she wants,' said Linda. 'No, it means she'll dance in *Swan Lake*, and the Director will notice her superlative talent, and—'

'Idiot!' interrupted Sonya, but her still pinker cheeks showed that Linda had guessed right.

Dave found his own hand taken in the gipsy's rough, dry fingers, turned and studied.

'You will never lack money,' Sonya interpreted.

'It does not take clairvoyance to recognize an American!' said Anton.

'You will not obtain everything else that you desire,' Sonya went on, 'but in the end that will be better for your happiness.'

It was obvious, easy stuff, thought Dave. You'd get much the same from any fair-ground booth back home. He was not surprised when Anton refused to put out his hand.

'It is ignorant superstition!'

The old woman gave him a long, straight look. Then she said something and went away.

'I did not like the way she said that,' said Sonya.

'What did she say?' asked Linda.

'She said, "Young sir, I would not foretell for anyone a future like yours".'

The others laughed, but a little uneasily. They could not help seeing that Sonya was upset. Anton made light of the incident. 'Sonya believes it all, good or bad,' he said contemptuously, refilling his glass and lighting one of his hollow-ended cigarettes. 'She has all the superstition that holds back our country. Even before she makes an entrance on the stage she must always cross herself as she waits in the wings!'

'All the girls do that! It is not the same – religion is not superstition!'

To his alarm, Dave saw that there were tears in her eyes. Really, Anton was too bad sometimes.

Luckily there was a diversion just then and the awkward moment was forgotten.

A table opposite them had stood empty all the evening. Now three men were shown into the box. One of them caught Dave's attention.

Even in that bizarre gipsy setting he made a remarkable figure. He wore an embroidered blue silk blouse and what looked like velvet breeches. Still more striking than his costume was his face, coarse and puffy, with lank hair parted in the middle and falling to his shoulders, a dark mat of beard, and eyes that roved round the whole room with a piercing intensity. Dave could have taken him for one of the performers, another fortune-teller maybe, but he was clearly a customer. He was welcomed like royalty, but he brushed past the obsequious waiter with an uncouth gesture and sprawled over a chair, elbows on table, leaving his two companions to find their own places. Champagne was waved away. A bottle of darker wine was set before him.

'Who on earth is that guy?' Dave whispered.

'That,' murmured Anton with suppressed venom, 'is the true ruler of Russia. At last you see him with your own eyes.'

'Gee, you mean – Rasputin?'

'Sh!' begged Sonya. She seemed almost to shrink into herself, like a flower closing at the onset of darkness.

They all stared across, over the heads of the gipsies crazily fiddling and strumming in the centre of the room. It seemed to Dave that Rasputin was staring back. He had the most eerie gaze, magnetic and penetrating.

So this was the man he had heard so much about since his arrival in Petersburg! Legend, gossip, rumour . . . how much was fact?

Rasputin, Anton had said, was a drunken illiterate scoundrel from the depths of Siberia, who posed as a *starets* or holy man. Ten years ago he had appeared at court and in some inexplicable way – magic, some declared, hypnotism, said others – he had saved the life of the little Tsarevitch, the Emperor's delicate only son and heir, when all the doctors were helpless.

Since that day, he had dominated the Tsarina, who revered him as a miracle-working saint and would not hear a whisper against him. According to Anton, the Tsar did what his wife told him, the Tsarina listened only to Rasputin. So it was now Rasputin who caused ministers and generals to be dismissed and put his own favourites into their places. To earn his enmity meant the ruin of one's career. His whispered recommendation guaranteed power and promotion.

If he was the most feared man in Russia he was also the most hated. The capital hummed with the scandals of his private life, his orgies of drunkenness and worse. But the Tsarina, keeping her court fifteen miles away at Tsarskoe Selo, closed her ears to the reports from Petersburg. It was all malice, all jealousy. It was what holy men had always had to suffer from lesser mortals.

Studying that face across the smoke-hung room, Dave could believe all Anton had told him.

'Let us go,' said Sonya faintly.

'It is still early,' objected Anton. 'Things are becoming more interesting. To one who studies politics—'

'That dreadful man,' she insisted. 'Those eyes . . . all the time I think he is looking this way.'

'You're right,' said Linda. 'He gives me the shivers.'

They argued for a minute or two. Anton could be terribly stubborn. The waiter suddenly appeared behind them and said something. Sonya let out a little scream. Dave thought she was going to have hysterics. Anton went dark with fury. He kept shaking his head and pouring out a torrent of Russian. The waiter persisted.

'What's the row about?' Dave asked.

'It is outrageous! He brings a message – an invitation – from that scoundrel over there—'

'*Anton!*' Sonya implored him.

'I do not care! He tells the waiter to bring the girls to his table. I tell the waiter to answer him, this is not Baghdad, he is not the Caliph, the girls are ladies under our protection—' The wine had increased Anton's normal eloquence.

The gipsy showed no sign of departing with this message. Dave glanced quickly across the room to the bearded face watching them. He did not like the expression on it. He stood up and said quickly:

'Tell him, thanks, but they have to be going.'

'Yes, yes,' said the girls eagerly, pushing back their chairs.

'No, it is cowardly to make that excuse!'

'It's commonsense,' said Dave tersely. 'Don't be so dumb. Come on, everybody.'

He bundled the girls in front of him. They were willing enough. The gipsy protested. Dave brushed him aside.

'Take care of this guy,' he told Anton over his shoulder. 'You got plenty for the bill? I want to stick close by the girls till we're out of here.'

Somehow they got down the steps, avoided a flouncing dancer, reached the door and recovered their coats. He was relieved to find Anton looming up behind them.

Thankful to be so well out of a nasty situation, he tried to steady Sonya's nerves by making a joke of it.

'I guess the old witch was right with one of her forecasts,' he said as he helped the girl into her coat. 'You certainly *did* attract the attention of a great personage!'

'David! It is not funny!'

Nor was it. For, as they turned to go, Rasputin stood there, swaying rather tipsily, like a grotesque bear and almost as massive.

'*Mademoiselle!*' he growled. '*Mademoiselle!*'

'Beat it!' Dave's words might have applied to anybody or everybody. The girls acted on it, and pushed their way frantically out into the night. The man flung out his arms. He was too late to clutch them, but he still barred the boys' escape.

Dave did the only thing possible. He punched hard into that silken blouse, ducked and dived through the doorway.

Behind him, the holy man let out a most unholy cry.

CHAPTER SEVEN

The Pistol and the Bomb

'Over here!' called Linda from the darkness. 'I've found a taxi! Quick!'

She was a good person to have around in an emergency.

Dave stumbled towards her through the rutted snow. They all piled into the taxi. The driver took an age to get the engine started. Dave watched the tavern door in an agony of suspense, but mercifully, no one seemed to be following them. They huddled tensely, silent until the taxi turned into the road and headed for the centre of the city.

'Beastly creature!' said Linda. 'I was terrified he'd come out after us!'

'David Davidovitch stopped that,' said Anton, and gave a highly exaggerated account of Dave's punch, making it sound like something heroic.

'Bunkum!' Dave was embarrassed. 'It wasn't more than a poke – a guy his size wouldn't have noticed it, only I guess he'd had a lot of liquor and it caught him off balance. Maybe the gipsies managed to head him off. They wouldn't want trouble, would they?'

'It is a pity,' cried Anton, 'that you did not have a knife in your hand!'

'*Anton!*' Linda sounded horrified.

'I mean it.'

'You are drunk!'

'I am not drunk.'

That was true enough. He never had been. The champagne had made them all more excitable than usual, but no more than that. The last quarter of an hour had brought them down to earth again.

'What is more,' went on Anton, 'I will explain why – I will give you a logical justification on moral grounds.'

'Not now you won't,' said Linda fiercely. 'Not in the taxi, my lad.'

'That's right,' said Dave in a warning tone, 'skip discussion till we get home.'

He guessed what was in Linda's mind. Anything they said might be understood by the driver, and, if so, reported to the authorities. He searched his memory. Had anyone mentioned Rasputin by name? He was pretty certain they hadn't. In which case, even if the taximan knew English, he would think it had been only an ordinary row in a gipsy tavern, not worth mentioning.

'I told him to drop us in the Nevsky,' murmured Linda. 'I thought a little walk might be better for our health.'

'But—' Sonya began, then stopped. Dave guessed that Linda had nudged her in the darkness. She sure had her wits about her, that English girl, he decided. She'd not only spotted the taxi, she'd remembered even in the heat of the moment not to go shouting the address of the Pension.

The taximan stopped where she had told him, some distance from their own turning. Dave counted out the roubles in the lamplight and the man drove off down the long thoroughfare. The four young people turned the other way, linked arms, and hurried home. Apart from anything else, the short walk gave them a chance to discuss how much they should tell Madame.

'The truth,' said Sonya quietly. 'Babushka and I under-stand each other. If there was deceit I could not live with her.'

'Anything you say,' said Dave. 'She's your grandmother, not ours.' For himself, he preferred it that way. Anton made no demur, now that the evening was safely over. It would have been different if they had told Madame beforehand, he reasoned, thereby putting an unfair respon-sibility on her. Madame was doubly answerable for Sonya, both to the Ballet School and to the girl's parents in Novgo-rod. But she would forgive the boys if they confessed now, and explained that the girls had not known where they were being taken.

Yasha opened the street-door to them, raising his eye-brows as they filed giggling past him. Now the tension was relaxed, they all felt a little light-headed. Anton stumbled on the stairs and the others had to haul him to his feet.

Yasha raised his eyebrows again, watched them out of sight, and shot the bolts again with disapproving violence. This, he seemed to indicate, was no way to go on.

Madame took the news of their encounter very well.

'One cannot foresee these things,' she said sensibly. 'If Sonya is to have a career in the theatre she must learn to cope with the uglier sides of life. That is true for all of us. I am sure that Lord Tintern would feel the same about Linda. But – since the man was Rasputin – I thank God that you all escaped so easily.'

Rasputin was the main topic at dinner the next evening. Madame had never set eyes on him, herself. Miss Upton rather surprisingly had.

'He came to dinner one night when I was at the Prince's – it was before the war, of course. A beast Madame Mitrova! Forgive me, he was nothing but a beast! His table manners – well, he *had* no table manners. And his general behaviour! No lady was safe with him . . . I would sooner have gone into a cage with a bear.' Miss Upton blushed deeply. The young people sat round the table all agog. This promised to be one of the old lady's more interesting anecdotes, and certainly not one of her nursery stories. But to their disappointment she broke off abruptly. 'Naturally, the Prince would never have him in the house again. But it made trouble, great trouble. The poor Tsarina was furious—'

'With Rasputin?' Dave asked.

'No, no. With the Prince. He was not invited by the Tsarina after that. It was the beginning of the coldness between them. You see, with the Tsarina this man manages to behave himself, so she cannot believe the stories about him. Of course, Rasputin could never behave like a *gentleman* – but in her presence he keeps sober and controls himself. She forgives his roughness because he is only a peasant – and, as she says, what were the Apostles but peasants and fishermen? It is a shame to think of her being so imposed upon, but there it is. She really believes that he saved her little boy, and that the Tsarevitch's life still depends upon him, so can you blame her?'

Mr Zorin had also seen Rasputin. Many times, he added. He contributed a startling piece of information: Rasputin was almost their neighbour.

'Neighbour?' echoed Sonya, wide-eyed.

'Certainly. He too lives just off the Fontanka.'

'He doesn't live at Court then?' said Dave.

'No, no. He prefers his freedom.' Mr Zorin lit his pipe

and twinkled through the smoke. 'He has a small flat. In Gorokhovaya Street. Number sixty-four to be exact.'

'How do you know this?' demanded Anton.

Mr Zorin shrugged. 'One picks up the gossip. And it is no secret. The main staircase is guarded by police. Though I can imagine that there is a back way if he wishes to slip in or out unnoticed.'

'Gorokhovaya Street,' said Anton huskily. 'To think that the swine is as near as that . . .'

'Young man,' said Miss Upton grandly, 'as a student of English you should learn not to use that word in polite conversation.'

'I'm sorry. But that man is not fit to live. For the sake of the country, somebody should do something about it!'

'Sh!' begged Madame. 'Anton Ilyitch, you say the wildest things. Even in private, you should not say such things.'

But Anton had mounted his high horse and there was no stopping him.

'I am not concerned just with "saying things" Madame. Plenty was said in public in the Duma the other day. I was there at the Tauride Palace, sitting in the public gallery. I heard Rasputin openly denounced. What good has it done? The Tsar does not listen to the politicians in the Duma. They are powerless. He gives every key position to the man Rasputin nominates. Look at our new Minister of the Interior – could anyone be less suitable for the post? But all the world knows, Rasputin said he was to have it, and the Tsar gave way. The "Little Father" indeed!' Anton almost spat out the traditional title in his anger. 'Nicholas the Second, "Tsar of All the Russias"! I tell you this, he cannot rule his wife, much less his empire. The Tsar is a puppet. Rasputin pulls the strings. It is time some patriotic Russian put a bullet into him.'

There was a shocked silence round the table. Mr Zorin broke it. His slow, deliberate voice brought them down to earth again.

'Our young foreign friends must not get the wrong idea,' he said gently. 'Anton Ilyich is not, I am sure, *recommending* assassination—'

'How do you know I'm not?' blustered Anton.

Mr Zorin ignored the question. 'But we are not perhaps so unaccustomed to it as you are in the West. More than one of our Tsars, and many people of rank, have perished in this way. It is only five years since the Prime Minister was assassinated in the opera house at Kiev, in the presence of the Tsar and his daughters—'

'*That* was outrageous,' said Miss Upton. It was not obvious whether it was the murder that had upset her or its happening in full view of young ladies.

'The pistol and the bomb are the traditional Russian gestures of protest,' said Mr Zorin.

'What else is left,' Anton demanded, 'when there is no political liberty? I ask you: can we *vote* to get rid of Rasputin? You know we cannot. Therefore, I tell you, there is only one way to save Russia—'

'That is enough for tonight,' said Madame.

Mr Zorin chuckled amiably and supported her in quelling Anton's rebellious objections.

'The debate is closed, my boy. And now, if you will all excuse me, I must finish a letter and take it to the post.'

CHAPTER EIGHT

The Night of Swan Lake

In the hallway the telephone shrilled. Madame Mitrova fluttered out to answer it. She had been on edge, expecting the call. She plucked the receiver from its hook.

'Sonya?'

'Yes, *babushka*!'

'You have good news? You sound happy!'

'I am so excited! It is just announced. I am to dance one of the *divertissements* in Act Three – the mazurka!'

'Wonderful! I am so happy for you, my darling! It is a beginning—'

'You will come, *babushka*?'

'Let them try to keep me out!'

'I must go now – we are not supposed to use this telephone—'

'Goodbye, then. Congratulations from us all!'

'Not yet, *babushka* – I may be terrible! Goodbye.'

The line died. Madame hung up and sailed back to the others. Her ivory cheeks were flushed with elation.

'It was our little Sonya, at the School! The Director is pleased with her, evidently. She is to take part in the production of *Swan Lake*. And in the masquerade scene at the castle she will have her own moment of glory!'

'I bet she's thrilled,' said Linda.

'Naturally! The child lives for her dancing.'

'Gee, this is something to celebrate,' said Dave.

'Later – we hope,' Madame agreed with a smile. 'But Sonya is nervous—'

'The nervous are the best,' said Mr Zorin genially.

'Yes! To achieve the heights it is necessary to have temperament.'

It was resolved that they must all somehow get in to the first performance. Even Mr Zorin, who seldom went to the theatre because it meant going without his beloved pipe, declared that he would not miss such an occasion for the world.

Tickets would be in great demand, but with Sonya in the cast, and Madame's privileges as a one-time member of the company, there would be no difficulty. The three elders would have stalls. The young people would be up in the gallery, affectionately known as 'Paradise', where, Anton insisted, all the really intelligent ballet-lovers were to be found.

The ballet was to be presented shortly before Christmas – or, as Linda and Dave insisted, just *after* Christmas. For, thanks to the discrepancy between the Russian and the Western calendars, they would this year enjoy two Christmasses.

Their own came first. There was mail from their families, with cards and presents and all the news from home. Linda's presents were simple and small: it was not possible to send much from England, for in that war-weary island, blockaded by the German submarines, there was a shortage of everything, though conditions were nowhere near so bad as in Russia. Dave's parents, however, were able to send him a luxurious food parcel, and there were wild scenes of rejoicing in the Pension when he opened it and handed round the contents. Real coffee, which he gave straight to Madame ... sugar ... and iced cake, dark inside and glistening with rich fruit ... candles ... cookies ...

'*It would have done you good to see their faces,*' Dave wrote home happily. '*Mom picked all the right things to send. Here in Petersburg a small bar of chocolate costs up to ten roubles – that's around a dollar – and you're lucky if you can find any.*'

Madame had nobly offered to attempt a special dinner so that the two young Westerners could celebrate their own Christmas.

'You have perhaps traditional dishes you eat? You know how things are with us – but something there perhaps is, that we could find in the shops?'

'It is all in Charles Dickens,' interposed Anton. 'But it is not in the shops of Peters, I can tell you that! Not this year!'

'Please don't bother, Madame,' said Linda, embarrassed. She knew it would tax all Madame's ingenuity to collect a few extra luxuries for the Russian Christmas two weeks later. 'As a matter of fact, the nurses are getting up a little party at the hospital. Lady Sybil says I can take Dave along. So we'll be fixed up for our own Christmas dinner, thank you very much.'

In the end, the young people did not do badly. Linda went to another, rather grander, affair at the British Embassy – Lord Tintern's daughter, however young, could hardly be left out at such a time. And Dave was invited to a free-and-easy gathering at his own Embassy, and was able to take Linda with him. The superior young Mr Hayes took them under his wing, paying great attention to Linda, especially when he discovered that she was an Honourable.

Linda herself was much more impressed by Jordan, the Ambassador's splendid black butler.

And two days later came *Swan Lake*.

Linda came rushing home from the hospital. Dave would have thought she had ample time to change for the theatre. But, when it came to changing, girls somehow never had enough time.

'Where's Anton?' she asked.

'He's not back yet.'

'Another of his student meetings, I s'pose!' Linda made a face. 'Really, that boy! He's been out three evenings running – out till all hours!'

'He won't miss Sonya's great moment.'

'I'll wring his neck if he does. The poor kid would be heart-broken. Oh, he is the limit! When he gets with his political pals he loses all sense of time.'

'Well, he has his own ticket. He can meet us at the theatre.'

'Looking like a scarecrow! Ah well, I'll look like one myself if I don't do something about it.'

Linda dashed upstairs and banged her door. Dave went to his own room more sedately. He had only to wash, change into a clean shirt and dark suit, and comb his hair. He did not yet need to shave every day. He was downstairs again before anyone else was ready.

The telephone rang. He had enough confidence in his Russian now to answer it. It was Anton, however, and he dropped into English when he recognized Dave's voice.

'David, I am exceedingly sorry—'

'*I* know – you're going to be late!'

'I may not be able to get to the theatre at all.' Anton sounded ill at ease.

Dave gasped. 'You mean, you're not going to be there to see Sonya?' He could not believe his ears.

'I cannot help it. Believe me, I am more disappointed than I can say.'

Dave could tell that Anton was upset. But it wasn't good enough.

'Say, what goes on?' he demanded.

'I – I cannot explain now. Not over the telephone.'

'I must tell Madame something. I suppose it's another of your late nights?'

'Yes, tell her that, will you? With my profound apologies?'

'Okay,' said Dave, not trying to hide his disgust.

'Tell her something else—'

'Yep?'

'I may be so late I shall not come home tonight. She must not worry. I shall sleep at a friend's. His room is much nearer to the University.'

'I'll tell her. And I'll tell *you* something when I see you!'

Dave hung up with an impatient gesture. It would be a nice thing for Sonya to hear, that Anton had put one of his College meetings before this historic evening in her career! Luckily the kid wouldn't know, as she danced, that he wasn't with the rest of them out in front, rooting for her.

What a crazy guy Anton was, he reflected! You couldn't help liking him but you couldn't help getting mad at him from time to time. He was so full of ideals and enthusiasms. He'd only to hear some stirring orator or read some new book, and he practically went up in flames. It might be all very fine for mankind and the cause of liberty, justice, democracy, and all that. But it was kind of hard on Anton's friends.

It was the first time Dave had been inside a Russian theatre.

The imperial opera house was huge and splendid. Looking down from their lofty perch in the gallery upon all that gilt and velvet, those curving balustrades, those ranks of boxes like holes in some gigantic and luxurious dovecote, Dave and Linda could well believe that it held two thousand people, and that on this important occasion every seat was filled.

Except, of course, one. Anton's place was empty on Linda's left, and they both knew in their hearts that he would not arrive, even by the interval.

A steady hum rose from the well of humanity below them. The white-tied musicians were filing into the orchestra pit and tuning up their instruments against the background of a thousand voices.

'Miss Upton is grumbling to Madame,' Linda guessed with a laugh. She mimicked the governess's precise speech. ' "Of course, it is not like the gala nights in the old days – when I was at the Prince's, don't you know? Such pretty dresses then, real elegance – even little me!" '

'You bet she is! But it looks okay to me.'

Their neighbours in 'Paradise' might be shabby, but, down below, the more expensive seats glittered with tiaras and pendants, and the splendid uniforms of the officers, bright with orders and medals, competed with the gayest of the evening gowns. Many of the men were elderly. With their beards and side-whiskers they looked, Dave thought, like left-overs from the previous century. The bare shoulders of the ladies were matched by the bald skulls of their escorts.

'Quite right too,' said Linda severely. 'The young ones ought to be at the front – not that they all are, by any means.'

No one was more magnificent than the attendants. Their red and gold liveries bore the imperial eagle in black, a reminder that the opera house, like the four other main theatres in Petersburg and Moscow, was under the direction of the Government. If Sonya completed her training and passed her final examination, she would join the company on a small salary and would be a public servant like any clerk in a ministry. But that wouldn't go on for ever, Linda explained. If Sonya was a success she would be able to pick and choose. She might stay here and become a ballerina, beloved and idolized. Or she might go abroad and dance for Diaghilev, the stormy genius who, since his dismissal from this theatre, had been electrifying western audiences with his own productions of Russian ballet. She might even become an independent international star like Pavlova . . .

Linda's rosy prophecies were cut short by the slow dimming of the immense chandelier overhead. The hem of the curtain glowed with light, the babble of the audience was hushed, the conductor tapped his baton, and the opening bars of Tchaikovsky seemed to draw the whole house together in breathless expectancy.

Act One showed a forest glade, with gold and russet trees and a romantic Gothic castle in the distance . . . There was a melancholy prince named Siegfried, his jester in green and apricot satin, his friends dancing and revelling ... then, when they had swirled away, leaving him on an empty stage, came the wild swans ...

Dave watched intently. He had never seen any ballet, everything was new to him, all the finer points mysterious and incomprehensible. He had heard Sonya discuss them with Madame. Technical terms, French mostly, had been bandied to and fro across the dinner-table: *battement, entrechat, fouchetté, arabesque* and dozens more. The regular ballet-goers apparently knew them all and they could criticize the dancers' technique as if they were baseball players back home. Dave knew he would never master the jargon himself. He could only sit back and enjoy the beauty, the colour, the lithe, effortless movement, held in that enchanted pool of light upon the stage.

'I couldn't spot her – could you?' he confessed as the curtain came down.

'No. Too many of 'em – I should have borrowed some opera-glasses.'

It was hard, from the remoteness of the gallery, to identify one face among so many dancers, especially when they flowed across the stage so rapidly.

'Never mind,' he said. 'We can't miss her special bit in Act Three.'

'No. She'll be dressed in Polish costume for that. Oh, Lord, this is when they play all the national anthems—'

The conductor stood up in the fully-lit auditorium and tapped his baton again. Each of the Allies had to be honoured. There were the anthems of Serbia and Rumania and Italy and Belgium, though nobody knew which was which. For France there was the *Marseillaise*, though (Linda explained afterwards) the Tsar and his ministers disliked it, because it reminded people of revolution. *Rule,*

Britannia! was always played, however, because *God Save the King* was considered a German tune. Finally they got to *God Save the Tsar*, and it was possible to sit down again or move around.

'People are getting bored now with all these anthems,' said Linda. 'When the war started, they didn't realize how many countries would come in.'

'I guess they'd bear another minute if they could include *The Star-Spangled Banner*,' said Dave dryly. He had never felt so bad about his own country being still outside the struggle with Germany. It had brought it home to him, standing there beside Linda, as one anthem crashed out after another. Civilization was involved in the greatest conflict of all time, but America stood aloof; and he himself was set apart, whether he liked it or not, from all his new friends.

Now it was the second act, an eerie moonlit scene beside the lake, with the Owl Magician descending from his ruined tower to summon his magical flock. The *corps de ballet* filled the broad stage . . . thirty-two human swans, their smooth arms curving, stretching, rising, falling, fluttering like wings, to express the essence of Tchaikovsky's music . . . It was exquisite. But Dave, with his untutored taste, was impatient for Sonya's mazurka in the next act.

Another interval . . . They left their seats, managed to get lemonade. It was so hot in the packed auditorium. The other galleryites stood arguing fiercely. From what Dave could hear, they were discussing the dancers, the decor, every detail of the ballet. Would they be pulling Sonya to pieces in the next interval? He was both relieved and tantalized to know that, whatever they said in their vibrant, emphatic Russian voices, he would not understand more than one word in ten. He wanted to hear her praised, but he would hate to hear her criticized unkindly. And these gallery experts, he had been told, were merciless.

The bell rang. They returned to their seats. Anton's was, as they had expected, still vacant.

'This is it,' muttered Dave. He could imagine Sonya in the wings, petrified with nerves, praying silently, crossing herself as her entrance drew near.

The lights dimmed. There was a warning roll of drums, then silence. Dave heard a puzzled murmur from his neighbours. The drums, it seemed, were no part of Tchaikovsky's music. Nor did the curtains part – there was no more than a quiver as a single figure slipped through and faced the audience across the footlights, a solitary figure in evening dress. The manager flung up a hand to arrest attention.

'Ladies and gentlemen—'

Everyone craned forward. What had happened? Was the ballerina suddenly indisposed? Or was there good news from the front – some surprise victory?

'I have an announcement. The news has just been made public—' The voice, tiny but clear in the huge opera house, was tremulous with controlled emotion. 'I have to tell you, ladies and gentlemen – Rasputin is dead!'

If he had meant to say more, he was given no chance. Two thousand people sprang to their feet, men and women, young and old. They shouted, cheered, waved programmes. Then, without any apparent lead from any one, they began to sing, and after a moment's straggling hesitation the musicians seized their instruments and joined in.

This time the anthem seemed to shake the building. '*God save the Tsar!*'

The lights blazed up again. The chandelier glittered like a tree of diamonds. Dave saw that the people round him had cheeks streaming with tears. And they were tears of pure, terrible joy.

CHAPTER NINE

The Secret Police

'It *was* bad luck for Sonya,' said Linda afterwards as they hurried home through icy streets.

'Even worse luck for Rasputin,' said Dave grimly.

'I should think he deserved all he got – whatever he *has* got. But it was Sonya's first real chance – and nobody was in any mood to watch the dancing by then.'

It was all too true.

The announcement from the stage had shattered the spell. The audience had been brought back to realities. After their delirious outburst the performance had continued. The applause had been warmer than ever, they had seized every excuse to clap and cheer, but it was their country's deliverance they were celebrating, not the artistry of the dancers.

It was, as Linda said, bad luck for Sonya. The ball scene offered a succession of vividly contrasted dances. There were six princesses, pirouetting in their pale, bell-shaped skirts . . . then, as the masquerade grew more furiously gay, the bolder colours of the various national costumes, Venetian and Spanish, Hungarian and at last the Polish . . .

The mazurka was just one of the *divertissements*, but for a student it was a coveted opportunity. But who tonight would remember a new face or mark a new name on the programme? Even as his neighbours applauded, Dave

79

could read the thoughts that filled their minds: how did Rasputin die, what will happen now?

'I wish we were allowed to telephone her at the School,' said Linda, as they turned to follow the bank of the canal. 'Never mind, we must all write notes and congratulate her. I expect she'll be feeling rather flat now that it's over.'

'I've some chocolate left. I'll leave it at the School for her in the morning. It ought to be flowers, I suppose—'

'Chocolate will do her more good. I don't know how she gets up the energy for this dancing. It's jolly hard work. She's such a slip of a thing. And they're none of them properly nourished.'

'There speaks Nurse Lowdham.'

'Idiot!'

They had reached the Pension. Yasha opened the door with remarkable promptitude, as if he had been hanging about inside. Dave thought that he wore an odd look as he touched the peak of his cap and wished them goodnight. No doubt he had heard the news of Rasputin's death himself. It seemed to be all over the city. There had been drunk men singing about it as they walked along the Nevsky.

Upstairs, the outer door was ajar.

'Surely the others aren't back before us?' said Linda. 'They'd never get a cab in all that crowd—'

'There'd be more noise if they were home,' said Dave with a laugh, imagining the excitement and chatter. The Pension was silent, but, at the sound of their own voices, the door of the kitchen opened and the old servant peered out.

'*Mademoiselle!*' she quavered, and let out a torrent of incoherent and incomprehensible Russian.

Linda turned back. She had learnt the knack, with her wounded soldiers, of making her scrappy knowledge go as far as possible. She could usually deal with Anya. Dave was more self-conscious about getting his grammar and pronunciation right. So, though he worked harder at the language and by now had a sounder basis than the happy-go-lucky English girl, he was shy with the broad-spoken old countrywoman. Never dreaming that anything was seriously wrong, he continued up the last flight of stairs to his attic room.

He never reached it.

Anton's door, next to his own, stood open and there was a light on.

'Anton, you old devil!' he shouted and burst in. Then he stopped short, flabbergasted.

There was no sign of the student.

The room was in disorder. Every drawer had been ransacked. Books and papers had been tossed about and mingled with articles of clothing. Sheets and blankets had been heaped in the middle of the floor. Two men were prodding the mattress.

They straightened up at Dave's cry and turned to face him. He had never seen their faces before, but their green overcoats had an all-too-familiar look.

'Anton Korolenko?' one of them asked.

He thought they were asking whose room it was.

Instinctively he nodded. '*Da.*'

The detective said something in a clipped, formal tone. Dave gaped at him, wondering whether he had understood correctly or not. While he wondered, the second man stepped quickly up to him from the side. There was a double click, and he felt the metal cold round his wrists.

*

Anton had often said that the Ochrana could be very stupid, despite their elaborate organization. After that evening, Dave agreed with him.

It was in vain that he shouted explanations and denials, repeating his own name and '*Amerikansky! Amerikansky!*' Linda did no better. She appeared when they were leaving, and joined in Dave's protests, but the detectives stolidly ignored her and shouldered their way to the door. Old Anya was useless. She gibbered tearfully in the background.

Madame or Mr Zorin might have achieved something. But there was still no sign of them when Anton and his captors stepped out into the street. He heard Yasha shoot the bolts behind them. Too much was happening in Petersburg tonight for doors to be left unlocked.

Dave could get no satisfaction from his escort. To all his questions and explanations one man merely answered woodenly, 'We have our orders,' and, 'The inspector will decide.' His companion said nothing at all.

They walked for about ten minutes. It was late, and the side-streets were empty and silent. A chill midnight air blew round each corner. They came to a grim-looking building, with two uniformed policemen on guard, armed to the teeth as usual, with dangling swords to supplement their truncheons and revolvers.

Dave was taken into a dimly-lit reception-hall. It was crowded and depressing, rather like the worst kind of railway waiting-room. There were a lot of policemen standing round and plain-clothes detectives going in and out. Sitting on a bench or clustered round the charge-desk were about twenty men of various types. Some looked ragged and disreputable, several might have been clerks, five (as their caps showed) were University students. There was no sign of Anton.

An irritable official was writing with a squeaky pen. When Dave's turn came, he stifled all the boy's halting protests.

'Not now . . . There will be time for that in the morning . . . You see for yourself, I have all these other people . . .'

The handcuffs were unlocked. Dave had to turn out his pockets. Even the harassed policeman exclaimed admiring at the sight of his watch: Dave wondered if he would ever see it again. His money was counted. Unfortunately, when changing into his best suit for the theatre, Dave had not transferred his wallet containing his residential permit and his last letter from home. They would have established his identity and American citizenship, and then, surely, the stupidest official would have thought again? Alas, he had for once remembered his mother's dictum, Don't bulge out your pockets and spoil the line of your suit. He hadn't a scrap of documentary evidence to wave under the noses of the police, and whether he addressed them in broken Russian or fluent American they were equally unmoved. Maybe they thought he was just acting foreign to confuse them?

He was taken along a corridor, up some stone steps, and down another passage, lined with cell-doors. A door was unlocked, he was pushed inside, and the bolts shot behind him. The pale gaslight in the corridor, slanting through the iron grille, revealed a space measuring about four paces by three. It contained a plank bed with a straw mattress, several rough grey blankets smelling of disinfectant, and a pillow. A bucket in one corner was the only other furniture.

Dave was not one to shake the bars and scream. Clearly,

he would get no satisfaction out of these people until the morning. Then we'll see, he resolved grimly. For the next few hours he'd just have to make the best of it.

Gradually the building fell silent. The footsteps and the slam of doors died away. At long last, despite the bitter cold and the worrying thoughts that raced round and round in his head, he dropped into an uneasy sleep.

When he woke, everything looked just the same. The sickly gaslight still slanted through the grille in the door. There was a barred window opposite, much higher, quite beyond his reach. It looked ink-black outside. Without his watch, he could not guess how long he had slept.

Questions began to eddy in his mind, endless, unanswered. What had Anton been up to? Was it linked with Rasputin's death? And how had Rasputin died? Surely by some violent means, or why all this flurry of police activity? Last night it had looked like a general round-up of suspects, many no doubt as innocent as himself.

What would happen next? Somehow he must convince the police of his identity, his innocence. Get in touch with the American Embassy . . . He made a face, thinking how Mr Hayes would react . . . But it had got to be done. With luck, Linda or Madame Mitrova might have done so already.

The door was unlocked. A policeman tramped in. He put down a mug of tea and a hunk of black bread.

'Breakfast,' he announced.

'I am an American citizen,' said Dave slowly and with dignity. 'I wish to telephone.'

'It is forbidden for prisoners to use the telephone.'

'Can I have a pen and some paper?'

The man hesitated. 'For what purpose?'

'To write a note.'

'To whom?'

'The American Ambassador.'

'Until your case has been investigated you can write only to the police authorities. Have you complaints about your treatment?' The man scowled in a discouraging manner.

'Of course I have!' Dave retorted. Then he shrugged his shoulders, muttered in English, 'Oh, what's the use?' and began to eat his bread.

About an hour passed before the policeman returned, accompanied by the two detectives of the night before. They took Dave back along the passage, up another flight of stairs, and into an office. It was warm, and he was thankful for that. The gas was burning, but the dawn was rose and silver outside the window. And there were no bars.

Two men sat behind desks. The elder, bald with a white moustache, frowned at the report in front of him.

'Is it true that you are an American?'

'Yes, sir.'

'You understand Russian?'

'A little.'

The official turned to his colleague, a small neatly bearded man whose gold fillings flashed when he spoke. This man addressed Dave in passable English.

'The superintendent says it will be better if you are interrogated in your own language.'

'Fine! Then I want to know why—'

'Wait. It is for us to ask the questions. There is evidence here that you were arrested alone in the room of Anton

Korolenko, that at first you said you *were* Anton Korolenko—'

'I misunderstood your policemen.'

'You misled them.'

'Well, they must have realized I was an American, soon
as I opened my mouth.'

'It is easy to imitate a foreigner, to pretend that one
cannot speak one's own language properly. Our men know
no English – but they know that it is the subject Korolenko
studies at the University. They could not judge.'

'Okay, sir. But *you* can.'

The older man, who had been straining to guess the
general drift of the conversation, pushed a paper towards
the bearded one, pointed to something, and said in
Russian:

'He insisted that his name was Gopkins!'

Dave had long ago got used to that version of his name.
There was no 'H' in Russian. Anton sometimes studied a
textbook on Shakespeare's '*Gamlet*'.

'That's right,' he said. 'David Hopkins.' And he added:
'You can check with the Pension Yalta surely? My permit
is there in my other jacket.'

'Do not distress yourself, young man,' said the junior
official. 'We are satisfied on this point.'

'Then why don't you let me go? You've no right to
hold me here. There'll be trouble about this – jailing an
American citizen. Wait till the Ambassador—'

'One moment.' The Russian tapped his teeth with a
penholder. 'There is nothing sacred about being American.
You are not our allies. Many Americans sympathize with
Germany in this war.'

'Well, I don't!'

'I am glad to hear it. But as to detaining you last night,

our men had every justification. At the most, it was a misunderstanding, largely your own fault. I am sure your ambassador will see that.'

Dave swallowed hard. He would have liked to punch the bland face smiling at him across the desk.

'Can I go now, sir?' he said quietly.

'Not yet.'

'You mean – you're still holding me? I'm still under arrest?' His heart sank.

'Not exactly. Indeed, not at all. No, Mr Gopkins, I am asking you to stay a little longer – voluntarily – to assist us in our inquiries.'

'About what?'

'About your friend, Anton Korolenko.' The official drew a plain sheet of paper before him and prepared to make notes. 'You must know him quite well. You live at the same address. He would no doubt talk freely to you – the more freely because you are a foreigner. What, for example, are his political views?'

'I take no interest in Russian politics.'

'But Korolenko does!'

'There is nothing I can tell you. You had better ask him.'

'I should like to – very much. But at the moment he cannot be found. Where did he go last night?'

'I have no idea.'

'And the night before? And – let me see – ' The bearded man calculated – 'the night before that?'

'I don't know all his movements. If I did, why should I tell you?'

'Because, Mr Gopkins, this is not an ordinary murder case, but one of the highest political importance. The death of Rasputin—'

'So he *was* murdered?'

'You may know better than we do. But we have to assume that he was murdered. We are still looking for the body.'

'Oh,' said Dave in a subdued voice, digesting this fresh information. The mystery deepened. 'All the same,' he went on. '*I* can't tell you anything about it. Or about Korolenko. And as you say I'm only here voluntarily, I guess I'd like to go.'

'One moment, Mr Gopkins—'

'You've no power over me,' said Dave obstinately. 'You can't force me to say things.'

'No, but you would be wise to co-operate. You wish to remain in Russia?'

'I don't know that I do, all that much! But,' he added lamely, 'I guess my Dad wants me to.'

'Then consider. If you will not assist us, your permit can be withdrawn. You can be expelled.' The man smiled. 'Perhaps now you would like to talk a little about your friendship with Korolenko?'

'I'll be darned if I will!'

The telephone rang on the bald man's desk. He answered it. His tone instantly became respectful, almost servile.

'Yes, Excellency . . . As it happens he is here, now, Excellency . . . I was about to do so, Excellency . . . No, there need be no embarrassment, the department is covered, the explanation is quite easy . . . Yes, Excellency, without a moment's delay.'

All this Dave could follow plainly. And the man's next words, flung savagely across the desk at his colleague as soon as he had put down the receiver: 'Tell him he can go. It is an order. We have got to get him out of here!'

CHAPTER TEN

A Letter from Prison

'You have Rosalind to thank,' said Madame an hour later, pouring Dave a second glass of very welcome tea. 'Last night we were all distracted – we did not know what to do. It is difficult, you know, for us Russians. It is our government that does these things. I – I did not know what would happen if I telephoned your embassy. But Linda, she said, "I do not care – if necessary I will telephone the Devil himself!" She cares for nobody, that girl!' Madame smiled, but her face was haggard as though she had slept badly. 'So, late though it was, she telephoned. And clearly they must have taken quick action, or you would not be back here now.'

'And mighty glad!' said Dave. 'Any news of Anton?'

'No. The naughty boy!' Madame shook her head sadly. 'I ask myself, where is he, what has he done, up in what is he mixed? These students! If they would apply themselves to their own studies, as we dancers do – but no, it is all the time politics, revolution, revolution! Always in Russia it has been the same. But I think it gets worse now, every year.'

The next few days were a time of restless anxiety in the Pension. What had happened to Anton? Could he conceivably have been mixed up in the murder of Rasputin?

Murder it was. Of that there was no doubt. Divers had recovered the body from the river. It bore bullet-wounds and marks of savage battering. It had been dropped through a hole in the ice, the assassins hoping no doubt that it would not be found until the spring thaw, if then. But it was as though the dead man, who had dominated the country in his life, refused to disappear so easily.

There were few people who spoke of the killers as 'assassins', however: to the vast majority they were heroes who had liberated Russia. They were cheered by the workers at factory meetings. Their health was drunk in the officers' mess of every regiment. For several evenings the theatre audiences repeated the demonstrations that had greeted the original announcement: over and over again they stood and sang *God Save the Tsar*. Even in the churches Rasputin's death was hailed with joy, and there were special *Te Deums* to offer thanks for it. Now perhaps the tottering nation could pull itself together. With honest government the war with Germany might yet be won.

'A strange thing happened at the hospital,' Linda confided to Dave. She had thought nothing of it at the time, but subsequent events had brought it back to her.

The hospital occupied only the first floor of the Grand Duke Dimitri's palace. The Grand Duke retained his apartments above, reached through a door leading to a private staircase. On the night before the *Swan Lake* performance Linda had seen him hand a key to Lady Sybil. She had caught the words, whispered but so emphatic as to carry to her ears: 'Please wear this round your neck – night and day – until I ask for it back.'

'It's rather odd, now,' said Linda. 'We've had the secret police round. They reckon they only want to put a guard on the Grand Duke for his own safety, but he won't let them in. Of course, if you're a Grand Duke even the Ochrana can't push you around! Then we had another set of visitors trying to get into the palace – they made out they wanted to see the patients, but we saw through that, because they couldn't tell us any of the names of the wounded. We're pretty sure they were some of Rasputin's lot. Anyhow, Lady Sybil booted them out – she's got a wonderful way with her,' Linda added admiringly.

'Do you think – do you think the Grand Duke is hiding someone upstairs?'

'Well, there's something fishy going on. I mean, why all this interest? What was that key he gave to Lady Sybil?'

'Lord,' said Dave anxiously. 'I hope *you* won't be the next one to land in the cells!'

'That'd be something to tell Mummy, wouldn't it?' Linda looked cheerful at the prospect. 'Don't worry, Dave. There isn't going to be any funny business at the hospital. We've got a military guard of our own now. The Governor sent them – special request of the Prime Minister. Oh, we're *very* superior, we have friends in high places.'

'Talking of high places – if there is somebody being hidden upstairs, I wonder who it is. What if it was Anton?'

'That would be a lark!'

'It might mean he was a murderer,' Dave reminded her grimly.

'I don't think our Anton could kill a fly – if it came to the pinch!'

Later that day a uniformed policeman came to the Pension.

Anton Korolenko was under arrest.

For the moment he was not allowed to send letters or receive them. But if Madame would make up a parcel, with towel, soap, a clean shirt, and other permitted items, it would be passed on to the prisoner.

Suddenly, Rasputin's name disappeared from the newspapers.

It was so abrupt, so universal, that every one knew it was by order of the censors. It was the first time that Dave had been aware of the censorship. Not just the war news but everything had to be passed by it in Russia, even in time of peace.

This clamp down, overnight, of the mere mention of Rasputin was clearly a high-level decision. But what did it mean? What was happening?

'You expect to know, because you are American,' said Madame.

'Sure! Back home, the newspapers—'

'It is different in Russia. We are not told these things.'

Dave thought it was extraordinary.

Linda picked up news and rumours from the hospital. The Grand Duke was in disgrace with the Tsar – or at least with the Tsarina. He had been given an appointment in Persia, a polite kind of exile. He had left his palace, and his private apartments were no longer in a state of siege.

'I think I know who was being hidden there,' said Linda.

'Who?'

'His friend, Prince Yusopov. The story is that Rasputin was killed in the basement at the Prince's house.'

'Holy smoke!'

'The Prince did the killing. But the Grand Duke was there.'

'Do you believe this?'

'Well, one thing's certain – the Prince has been ordered

to get out of Petersburg. He's gone to one of his estates in the country. Sort of open arrest, I s'pose you'd call it.'

Soon everyone in the city was giving Prince Yusopov the credit for removing Rasputin. People knelt in the snowy street outside his palace to give thanks for his action. Linda saw others doing the same under the windows of the hospital. It certainly looked as though her own Grand Duke had been mixed up in it as well.

'But what about poor old Anton?' Dave complained. 'Say these aristocratic guys did it. All that happens is an order to get out of town. The Ochrana can't touch them. Even the Tsar is scared. But old Anton, who probably wasn't within miles and didn't know a thing about it – they hold him in a cell. And I know what those cells are like!'

It was hard to get any news of their friend. After much effort, Madame extracted a few crumbs of information.

Anton, it appeared, was just one of numerous people the police had rounded up on suspicion of being involved in the Rasputin murder, and then held because of their supposed links with forbidden organizations.

Anton's trouble was that, after insisting that he had a complete alibi for the night in question, he had changed his attitude and refused to say where he had been or with whom.

'I have seen a lawyer,' said Madame, 'in case it comes to a trial. He says the boy is obstinate—'

'No need to pay a lawyer to tell us that,' said Miss Upton. She was the least sympathetic of the party. She had little use for wild young men who spoke rudely of her beloved Tsar.

Madame ignored the interruption. 'He is sure that Anton was not concerned with the main affair, but it is possible that he was at some illegal meeting or in company with known revolutionaries.'

'It would be just like Anton,' said Linda. 'He would shield his friends, no matter what it cost him.'

'We must pray that it comes to nothing serious,' said Madame. 'It would break his mother's heart.'

Days dragged by and became weeks. Anton was neither released nor brought to trial. He was, however, allowed to write letters. He sent a general letter to Madame, with messages for everybody. He was not permitted to write in a foreign language, anyhow. As he could not discuss his case, the letter was not very informative.

'*I am fairly well*,' read Madame, translating as she went, '*but because of my chest the prison doctor has moved me into the infirmary. It is warmer there and the food is better. We even have milk! Take note of that, my friends – they allow us milk.*' Madame looked up from the letter and smiled in a rather puzzled way. 'I do not know why he lays such emphasis on the milk.'

'Anton hates milk,' said Linda.

'Then it must be meant as a joke, I suppose,' said Madame doubtfully. She finished the letter. Anton sent love to everybody and inquired about Sonya's dancing. It was odd to realize that, until he received their reply to his letter, he would still not know how the performance had gone off all those weeks ago.

Afterwards, when they were alone, Linda said to Dave: 'Do you think you could get hold of that letter?'

'Anton's? Why?'

'Just an idea.'

'Why don't you ask Madame yourself? She'd let either of us borrow it. There's nothing secret about it.'

'I'm not so sure. It would be better if *you* asked. You

could make out you wanted to make yourself a translation
or something.'

'Okay,' said Dave, rather mystified.

'Make it sound natural.'

'Sort of casual? I get you.' And, though Linda would say
no more just then, he was beginning to get a glimmering of
the idea at the back of her mind.

Why Anton's emphatic mention of milk – when apparently he did not like the stuff? Dave had read somewhere
that milk was one of the liquids you could use, at a pinch,
for invisible writing when the proper chemicals weren't
handy. Linda might know about that kind of thing through
that odd mother of hers who went to prison for the sake
of women's rights.

He borrowed Anton's letter without difficulty. It was
afternoon, Miss Upton taking a nap on her bed, Mr Zorin
out at business, Linda just in from hospital. They had the
room to themselves.

'You're supposed to heat it,' said Linda, taking the sheet
of cheap grey prison paper and holding it in front of
the stove.

'Something's coming!' he exclaimed.

'So it is!'

'It's very faint—'

'But you can read it! Look!'

She held out the paper. Across the lines of purple hand-
writing it was just possible to decipher a few words in pale
brown letters, printed with apparent difficulty. But at least
they were in English. In a low voice Dave read: '*Beware
Z – not what seems.*'

'Zorin!' said Linda with a little gasp.

'He's the only "Z" we know.' Dave thought for a
moment. 'He couldn't be a police spy?'

'Oh, *not* our Mr Zorin!'

'What else would Anton mean?'

'But did he ever say anything? I mean, before he disappeared – before anything happened?'

'No. But he might have heard things – from other prisoners, say. Mr Zorin was there when he said all that wild stuff about Rasputin deserving to be killed—'

'What an awful thought!' The girl was thoroughly roused by now. 'Suppose we have got a disguised policeman living here, listening to everything we say! We've got to settle this, Dave, one way or the other. We can't go on not knowing, sitting at the same table with him—'

'Well, we can't *ask* him.'

'Of course not – stupid! But there are other ways.'

'Here, where'ya going?'

'Up to his room! Just to take a look round. There might just be something that would give him away.'

'See here, Linda, you can't go—'

'No such word as "can't" – as Miss Upton would say! You needn't come if you're scared. But *she's* fast asleep, and Madame is out, and Anya's standing in line at the baker's. She won't be back for hours. But she hangs the keys in her broom-cupboard.'

Dave argued no more. They got the key they wanted and crept guiltily up to Mr Zorin's room.

It was a room like any other, just tidier than Dave's. Plain paper, envelopes, inkpot and pen were ranged on a bare table, ready for the next of those mysterious letters. The only mysterious thing about him, so far.

'Tobacco in the tin,' said Dave, checking.

Linda knelt at the chest of drawers. Careful though she was they squeaked alarmingly as she drew them open. She poked and lifted articles of clothing.

'He wears nightshirts,' she said, suppressing a giggle. 'I felt sure he would.'

There was nothing sinister about that. There was nothing sinister anywhere in the room. Very little at all, in fact, beyond the furniture. Mr Zorin seemed to have few possessions of his own.

She dragged out a battered trunk from under the bed. It was unlocked. There was no reason why it should be locked, for it was empty. Or was it?

'Hold it,' said Dave suddenly, as she was about to close the lid.

'What's wrong?'

'It doesn't look deep enough, somehow.'

Inside, the trunk looked oddly shallow. Dave tilted it to test its weight. It was oddly heavy, too, for an empty trunk.

'It could have a false bottom,' he grunted, kneeling and running his fingers round the inside. 'But can we figure out the trick of it, that's the question?'

'Oh, do try! But hurry!'

Linda was impatient. After a fruitless minute's fumbling, she begged him to give up. Her nerve was running out. She wanted to get out of the room. But Dave had the dogged persistence of the boy with a mechanical kink. He was more and more certain that there was something to work, more and more determined to solve the puzzle. At last he felt something hard under the fabric lining. It clicked at his finger's pressure. The whole bottom of the trunk moved slightly, like an inner lid.

'Dave, you *are* clever!'

'There we are,' he said, a little smugly. 'Quite smart, really.'

The false bottom hinged up to reveal another compartment about two inches deep. It was stuffed with papers, books and pamphlets. Words like 'Revolution', 'Social Democrat' and 'Bolshevik', leapt to the eye, in bold black exclamatory print.

It was not at all what they had expected. Nor was the soft-voiced greeting of Mr Zorin, stooping over them from behind.

'Well, my children – and what do you think you have found?'

CHAPTER ELEVEN

The Bolsheviks

It scarcely occurred to Dave to be frightened. Who could be frightened of Mr Zorin, so tubby, so benevolent, with his quiet pussycat movements and his cosy aura of tobacco-smoke?

Rather was Dave overwhelmed with shame, to be caught prying like that. His cheeks burned. So did the girl's. I could have *died*, she confessed afterwards.

It was not in their code. Nothing but Anton's message would have pushed them into such action. But to Mr Zorin it seemed nothing extraordinary. He closed the door gently and sat down on his bed.

'You say nothing? It was never so with Sherlock Holmes and Doctor Watson. Always they had much to say. And which of you is Sherlock Holmes? Which is Doctor Watson?'

'It was my fault,' said Dave quickly. Linda broke in with a contradiction, but he shushed her, and for once she subsided. 'I guess I owe you an apology, Mr Zorin. It was a misunderstanding—'

'So?'

Mr Zorin watched him impassively, more than ever like a huge, bespectacled cat.

'We—' Dave floundered, anxious not to betray the secret of Anton's letter. 'We sort of got the notion you

99

might be a police spy, and that it might be your fault Anton went to jail for what he said – about Rasputin and all that.'

'You thought that?'

'Course, we see now we were absolutely wrong—'

'Indeed? And why?'

'Well . . .' Dave pointed to the wads of leaflets and other literature tightly crammed into the bottom of the trunk. 'All this stuff. I guess you're right on the other side.'

Mr Zorin nodded. 'And now you have seen, what will you do?'

'Do?'

'Will you speak of this? To the police? Or to anyone?'

Dave and Linda looked at each other. 'It would be silly,' said the girl, 'if *we* became police spies.'

'Sure,' Dave agreed. He glanced down at the leaflets, spelling out some of the words. 'Does this mean,' he asked, 'that you're what they call a Bolshevik?'

Mr Zorin studied his expression, then nodded. 'Of course. The Bolsheviks are the only people who will get things done. That is what our young friend Anton has never realized. But he will learn by experience that we are right.'

'I don't understand Russian politics,' said Linda. 'All these names! Bolsheviks and Mensheviks, Social Democrats and Social Revolutionaries, Cadets and the rest of them! But we don't much like your secret police, and we certainly shan't go telling tales about a few books and papers.'

'Thank you, my dear. It would be inconvenient for me. It would mean a quick change of lodgings. I should have to go underground – there would be no difficulty, for we have a wonderful Bolshevik underground here in Peters –

but I am comfortable at Madame Mitrova's. I should miss all my good friends. And in spite of this – this little misunderstanding – I feel that you are still my good friends?'

'Oh, sure. Sure!' said Dave fervently.

'Good. Then – we forget everything? Not a word to anyone?'

'Rather!' Linda promised.

And so, harmoniously, the matter ended. Whatever Anton had heard in prison, he was clearly all wrong about Mr Zorin. It was just like poor Anton to go barking up the wrong tree.

People – simple people at least – had imagined that Rasputin's death would change everything.

There would be honest and efficient government. Rasputin's henchmen would be cleared out of the key posts he had found for them. The Little Father would reassert his power as emperor. The war would go better. Rasputin had been pro-German anyhow.

As things turned out, his removal seemed to make no difference at all.

They were terrible weeks, those first weeks of 1917. Frightful cold gripped the country. The temperature sank to forty degrees below zero. Trains came to a standstill as points and signals froze. The shops were emptier than ever as food supplies failed to come through.

Dave took his turn in the bread-lines. It was wrong that old Anya, or Madame herself, should wait all those hours on the sidewalk in the Arctic cold. It was as much as his own young blood could stand.

Listening to his neighbours in those endless patient

ranks, he felt close to the common people of Russia for the first time. He wrote to his father:

'*I guess something's got to bust, and soon. The folks here can take a lot, ten times what anyone would stand for back home. But there's a human limit.*'

His father asked for an 'assessment of the situation'. For all his high-level contacts with senators and bankers and editors, Mr Hopkins wanted Dave's view in Dave's words. Dave struggled to understand. He missed Anton to explain things – even if Anton's statements were apt to be wild and needed checking. Mr Zorin, he was pretty sure, could have told him a lot. But after that encounter in his room politics were never mentioned again. Mr Zorin certainly knew how to keep his mouth shut. If he was typical of the Bolsheviks, they must be more businesslike than Anton and his friends, who seemed to talk mostly and get themselves into jail.

'*If there is a revolution,*' he told his father, '*I can't see who's going to lead it. There aren't just two or three big parties here, as we and the British have. There seem to be lots of them, big and small, all disagreeing among them- selves. The "Cadets" is the short name for the Consti- tutional Democratic Party – they want something like the British system. The "S.R.", Social Revolutionaries, are the gun and dynamite boys – they favour assassination and red revolution, but I don't know whether they amount to a row of beans. The "S.D." are the Social Democrats – they want revolution, but they say you get nowhere just murdering individuals, and I guess this Rasputin business proves them right. The "S.D." are pretty well split among themselves: one wing is called the Mensheviks and the other the Bolsheviks. In Russian that means the "minority" and the "majority", but they got those nicknames when*

*they quarrelled way back, and right now I think there are
more Mensheviks than the other sort. And these are just
some of the groups.'* Dave frowned and sucked his pen.
*'I'm sorry if this isn't very plain, Dad, but it's not all that
plain to me. You can't just find things out in this country,
the way we would. Everything's censored. I guess that a
lot of the guys who matter most are either behind bars or
abroad in exile or floating round under false names.'*

Dave sealed his letter and took it along to the American Embassy.

There were times like this when he felt glum and homesick. What was the use, he asked himself? Russia was an impossible country. His father would be crazy to think of investing money here. In which case, what was he, Dave, doing here, month after month, enduring cold and discomfort and monotonous food, grinding away at a language that would never be any good to him?

And yet ... and yet ... something stopped him from dropping hints that he'd had enough, or asking straight out if he couldn't go home before his time was up.

Something made him unwilling to quit. Was it just that he had to prove himself to his father? Show that he could take it, that he was no softer than Dad had been at the same age? Was it something else too? A hunch that something was going to happen in this beautiful, menacing city – and a determination to see it through? Had Sonya even a little to do with his feelings?

He seldom saw her. She was kept hard at work at the Ballet School. It was seldom that she was allowed out to visit her grandmother. Madame might say that the rules in wartime were much slacker than they had been in her own young days, but they seemed strict enough to Dave. The place was like a nunnery, he said disgustedly.

'Oh, no, not a bit!' Sonya retorted. 'We are serious about our dancing, that is all.'

'You think of nothing else!'

'What else is there?' Her smile mocked him, but it was a kindly mockery. And he knew that she was only half jesting. She was not like ordinary girls. She was under a spell, just as much as any of the princesses in the ballets she took part in, only her spell was the theatre itself.

Her brief visits brought back a little gaiety to the Pension. Otherwise, with Anton missing too, it had become a sad place, with Miss Upton mumbling over her interminable games of ludo, Mr Zorin padding off to his room to write his mysterious letters, and Linda so tired by her hospital chores that she could hardly raise a smile. But when Sonya slipped in from school, sparkling with theatre news and gossip, demonstrating steps to her beloved *babushka*, and running her fingers over the long-neglected piano-keys, it was as though all the lights had gone up again on a shadowy stage.

Dave used to walk her to the Ballet School. It was usually the afternoon but already dark. The winter was old now, the stale snow crusted and discoloured, the ice grooved and worn.

'Is it cold like this in New York?' she once asked.

'Sometimes. Only outside. It's – it's warm indoors.'

He was almost ashamed to remember the comforts of home, the food, the brilliant lights, the fun . . .

'Tell me about America.' He tried. It was a big subject. 'And the theatres?' she prompted him. He could not tell her much about the theatres.

'Some day I want to see America,' she said. 'To dance there . . . Dave, when will this war be over?'

'Lord knows, Sonya.'

'Why does not America come in to finish it?'

'I guess that would take a lot of explaining,' he said awkwardly. 'Politics.'

He did not like to say that, though many Americans were sympathetic to the British and French, they hadn't much love of Russia. Tsar or Kaiser, Russian emperor or German emperor – what was there to choose between them?

'Oh, politics are so *boring*,' said Sonya.

'Sure. Sometimes. But, Sonya, I guess we got to make the effort – we got to try to understand—'

'You try then,' she said.

They had reached the School with its long colonnaded frontage. She paused at the door, under the haughty double-headed eagles of the Tsar. They clasped hands, continental-fashion, but it was too cold to remove gloves.

'*Au 'voir*, Dave. Thank you for seeing me home.'

She danced up the steps and into the building, as though she could hear music inaudible to other ears.

This is what she thinks of as 'home', thought Dave as he turned away, and I guess she's right at that.

CHAPTER TWELVE

Red Flags in the Nevsky

Now it was late February. Dave's diary, indeed, with its western dating, showed that March had begun. But in St Petersburg there was no let-up in the cheerless winter, no stirring hints of spring.

Anton had been in custody for two months. His case, like scores of others, was still 'under investigation'. Madame could not discover when, if ever, he would be brought to trial.

The authorities had their hands full. The city seethed with rumours of conspiracy. The Tsarina was to be seized ... the royal family were to be kidnapped ... the Tsar himself was to be arrested and forced to give up his throne ...

The Tsar was in fact still with the Tsarina, comforting her in her hysterical grief for Rasputin. Shut up on their country estate, blind and deaf to all that was going on, they might as well have been fifteen thousand miles away as fifteen. When the Duma opened its new session, the deputies in desperate mood, their president wrote to warn the Tsar that Russia was on the brink of revolution. The Tsar did not even reply.

When revolution was mentioned at the Pension Yalta, Miss Upton pooh-poohed the very idea.

'They have talked of revolution ever since I came to this

country,' she said. 'They will never do it. The Russians are religious. They love their emperor. It's a lot of silly talk. Students. And these dreadful strikers in the factories. But the Army will always be loyal. What can such riffraff do against the Army?'

What indeed, Dave wondered.

He knew that, apart from the police with their swords and revolvers, St Petersburg had a huge military garrison. 'More than a hundred and fifty thousand men,' said Mr Zorin, looking thoughtful – and looking also as if he had pretty accurate figures. It seemed a lot of men to keep in Petersburg, Dave reflected, when the Russians needed every man to stem the German advance into their country. And he had seen with his own eyes that, however short of equipment they might be at the front, there was no lack of artillery, machine guns and armoured cars in the capital. He had watched them on the parade-grounds or passing in columns down the Nevsky.

On the surface the Tsar's empire looked as strong as the ice on the river. Yet everyone knew it was only a matter of time before the ice cracked. Would it be the same with the emperor's power?

Nicholas must have felt that the City Governor had everything under control. For, on the very day that things began to move in Petersburg, he decided that it was time to resume his personal direction of the war. He ordered the imperial train and set out for the headquarters he had quitted two months before. They were at Mogilev, over four hundred miles to the south.

No one in Petersburg, of course, knew he had gone. It was coincidence that the riots began that day.

The women in the textile mills came out on strike. They trudged from factory-gate to factory-gate, gathering numbers as they went. Dave saw them in the afternoon, making for the heart of the city. From the Neva embankment he watched police massed on the bridges and forming a thin dark cordon across the ice. The people came flooding across from the industrial quarters, men as well as women, drab and ragged, the only colour provided by a few red flags and home-made banners. Twice the police beat them back with their truncheons. But, with the whole riverside frozen, it was too long a line to hold. At the third effort the crowd broke through. Dave saw them stream by, shouting and singing, battling their way to the Nevsky Prospect. Slogans were crudely daubed on their banners: 'DOWN WITH THE WAR!' and 'GIVE US BREAD!'

They chanted the same slogans, the vibrant Russian voices remorseless in their plangent rhythm, the broad grey faces terrible in their determination.

Yet nothing much happened that first day. Some bakeries were looted, some cobblestones and lumps of ice thrown. Nothing more. The police did not fire, the Cossacks were not issued with the whips they normally used against rioters, the troops kept out of sight in their barracks.

On the Friday and Saturday there were developments. 'The street-cars have stopped running,' Linda reported when she came in. At night Mr Zorin was away much longer than usual when he went to post his letter. 'It was no use to post it,' he explained. 'There is a general strike proclaimed – for three days.' Dave wondered if he had gone further, to deliver the letter himself. Of late Mr Zorin had been out a great deal in the evenings, no doubt at secret meetings with his Bolshevik friends.

They would have to be secret in future, anyhow. That day the newspapers carried the Governor's edict: all public meetings were banned and the strikers were ordered to return to work by Tuesday.

Dave smiled when he read the second instruction. It was only a three-day strike, due to end by Tuesday. 'I guess the Governor isn't feeling too sure of his authority,' he said.

'It's disgraceful!' snorted Miss Upton. 'He should adopt a firm line with these work-people.'

Linda heard at the hospital that the Governor had arrested a number of leaders including some of the Bolsheviks. Rumour put the total at a hundred or more. But Mr Zorin seemed quite unperturbed. He came in and out on his own business, soft of step and soft of voice, smiling and secret. No policeman rang the bell to ask for Mr Zorin. 'He's a smart one,' Dave murmured to Linda. 'He's the one they won't get wise to, not in years.'

On Sunday morning Sonya ran in to see her grandmother after church.

'It's awful!' she announced, wide-eyed. 'You can hardly get through the streets – such crowds, all pouring over from the Viborg Side. No one knows if the curtain will go up tonight. I don't know what things are coming to.'

'You are not dancing yourself, my dear?' asked Madame.

'No, but—'

'Then you will stay here, unless things quieten down.'

'*Babushka*, I couldn't! The Director—'

'If necessary I will telephone.'

'It will be quite safe to go. They are bringing out the soldiers.'

Sonya stayed until the middle of the afternoon. In that quiet side-street, behind their double-windows, they could hear no more than an occasional outburst of shouting from the Nevsky. They sat close round the stove, drinking tea in the gathering twilight, with just the tiny lamp in front of the sacred ikon, winking like a ruby. Sonya told them excitedly of another small part she was rehearsing in *The Sleeping Princess*.

She was a bit of a sleeping princess herself, Dave thought to himself as he listened. Some day soon she would wake up to the real world . . .

'*Babushka!* I must go!' She jumped to her feet. 'Yes, really – I shall be quite safe. Dave will escort me. Yes?'

'Sure!'

He went into the hallway, pulled on his overshoes, muffled himself against the bleakness outside. They went downstairs. Yasha saw them out with a familiar leer.

The darkness murmured uneasily. There was a background of myriad voices, rising and falling in the distance. As they approached the Nevsky they could make out the insistent chanting of slogans in unison. There was a new one now that Dave had not heard before.

'They are shouting, "Death to the German woman!" ' said Sonya breathlessly. 'They mean the Tsarina. Because she is German, you know. They blame her because the war has not been won.'

The Nevsky was a chaos of tossing banners. There was no traffic. The people flowed over roadway and sidewalks alike, men, women, children, workers, mingled with the well-to-do. There was no form of order. Vague groups and colours blurred with aimless strollers and obstructive knots of bystanders. It was a human sea, a restless sea of bobbing heads and thrusting shoulders, but a sea uncertain of direction, wavering at the turn of the tide.

'We'll never get through,' Dave panted. He kept tight

hold of her arm, lest he lose her in the throng. 'We should have gone by the side-streets—'

'Never mind – too late now – we'll manage somehow—'

'Whatever you say!'

'I don't see how there can possibly be a performance night. But at least I must get back to school.'

It was impossible to make headway. It was like swimming through treacle. Dave had one fear: Sonya must not be crushed among these immense men, her precious dancer's feet must not be trodden on by these clumsy boots . . .

'We had better march!' he cried.

She laughed. 'It is the only way!'

They slipped into a broad human current that seemed to be making, in a blind leaderless fashion, in the direction they wanted.

It was exhilarating, somehow, to be part of this stream, boiling along between the shuttered windows of the Nevsky, red flags straining in the gaslight, pale banners dipping and tilting like storm-wracked sails. The people were good-humoured, unfrightening. Rough, yes, haggard, scarred, pock-marked, dirty, under-nourished – but friendly. That Sunday, everyone out on the streets of Petersburg was accepted as a comrade.

It was exhilarating, too, to feel Sonya's arm linked tightly in his own, and to know that she depended upon him to protect her.

He bent his head to hers. He had to shout against the din, and her ear, because of the cold, was muffled by her round fur cap. 'All right?' he asked.

She smiled up at him. 'Of course!'

'There is no danger—'

'I am not afraid.' She squeezed his arm reassuringly.

Then suddenly, without warning, there *was* danger, grim danger, and his heart turned over inside him.

The people in front slowed, stopped. A few turned and tried to force their way back, clawing, shoving, stammering in urgent voices. But there were too many others pressing on from behind, unable to see the obstacle.

Dave caught the word, 'soldiers'. Rising on tiptoe, he strained to see ahead. He glimpsed the cold pale flash of slanting bayonets, the darker gleam of rifle barrels ... The troops were solidly ranked across the street from side to side ... And the crowd was being pushed against them, blindly, irresistibly, by the pressure from the rear.

Above the confused noises he heard the orders bellowed by an officer, the rattle of a hundred riflebolts as a hundred cartridges were rammed into the breech. He remembered that other Sunday Anton had often told him about, the notorious 'Bloody Sunday' in 1905 when, not a mile from this spot, the Tsar's troops had fired point-blank into the unarmed demonstrators, killing five hundred, wounding thousands more.

'We got to get out of here,' he grunted. He swung round, keeping firm hold of the girl. It was no good. The people behind were still crowding upon them, denser and denser. The warnings of those in front were lost in the general uproar.

There was no going back, no escape to right or left. They were penned, helpless, like cattle for the slaughter. His brain raced. What was best to do? When the shooting started should he drop flat, pulling the girl down beside him, trying to shield her? There was another danger though, perhaps worse than that of the bullets. If there was panic in that multitude, anyone who fell to the ground would be trodden to death. As well lie down in front of a stampede! No, at all costs he must keep Sonya on her feet. Risk the bullets. Run at the first chance. Maybe they could get into a doorway . . . any kind of shelter . . .

'*Fire!*'

The rifles cracked together, the bullets whined overhead. All overhead. For at the last moment, as if by a secret common understanding, all those menacing muzzles had swung skywards, every shot had gone singing harmlessly over the rooftops. There was an outburst of laughter and cheering from the front of the crowd. An officer was cursing, haranguing his soldiers.

Dave did not know it then, but it was an historic moment. The soldiers of the Tsar had disobeyed an order. They had not aimed at the men and women in front of them. They had refused to kill their fellow-countrymen.

Dave only knew that the peril had passed, the sudden intolerable tension mercifully broken. The crowd moved forward again, the soldiers stood aside. Ten minutes later he was able to deliver Sonya safely at the door of the Ballet School.

They had been lucky. It was not so everywhere in the city that Sunday afternoon.

There was blood on the steps of the Grand Duke Dimitri's palace. Dave had gone on there from the Ballet School, knowing that Linda was due to come off duty. It wasn't a time for her to walk through the unruly streets alone.

The British Hospital, usually so placid, was buzzing with excitement. A porter was swabbing down the staircase inside. There was a cluster of tearful women. Two English nurses were trying to pacify them. One turned and beckoned Dave.

'You're Linda Lowdham's friend, aren't you? You speak Russian?'

'Only a bit—'

'More than we do, I bet! Do try to make these women understand. The wounded are being taken care of. We shan't hand them over to the police. It's nothing to do with us. We aren't taking sides, we're just a hospital. The British Hospital.'

Dave did his best to translate. The women calmed down. They sat down on the floor, humbly and simply, like peasants in a field, to wait for whatever happened next. Linda came racing downstairs, dressed for outdoors. Her eyes lit up at the sight of Dave.

'Hullo! What are you doing here?'

'I guess you can do with an escort tonight.'

'I won't say no. We've had a day of it. But Sister says there's nothing more I can do just now.'

For the second time that afternoon Dave walked through St Petersburg with a girl on his arm. Linda chattered away, telling him what had happened.

There had been a riot in one of the big squares. This time the soldiers had obeyed orders and fired volleys into the crowd. At least a hundred people had been killed or wounded. Some casualties had been carried straight into the British Hospital. Linda had had her first experience of cases fresh from the firing line – the blood and the filth, the moans and laboured breathing, the low-voiced orders of surgeon and Sister, the abrupt and shocking silences of death.

'They kept me too busy to think much,' she confessed. 'I do feel a bit shaky now, though. It was sweet of you to come for me.'

CHAPTER THIRTEEN

The Fall of the Eagles

Next morning, Dave insisted on escorting Linda to the hospital.

They heard a military band in the distance. In a way the perky, brassy music was a comforting suggestion that conditions were returning to normal: the soldiers were drilling, instead of killing. On the other hand it perhaps sounded heartless after what had happened the day before?

'Listen!' said the girl as the music drew closer. 'That's odd!'

'What is?'

'They're playing the *Marseillaise*—'

'Why shouldn't they?'

'Remember, the powers that be don't like playing it – they still think it's revolutionary—'

'Do you see that?' he interrupted excitedly as they turned into the Nevsky and saw the marching column.

'Red flags!'

'And no officers! That's a sergeant leading them!'

Cheering crowds kept pace with the soldiers on both sides of the wide avenue. A grinning youth answered Dave's question. It was the Volinsk Regiment, he said. They were marching to the other barracks to bring out the Litovsky Regiment and the rest of the garrison. By dinner-time, with any luck, they would all have come over to the side of the strikers.

'I guess it's gone beyond a strike,' Dave said to Linda as they walked on.

He delivered her to the hospital and decided to take a walk around the city. He felt tense and restless. It was no morning to go back to the Pension and bury his nose in books. Things were moving, and fast. Dad would want to know what was happening. He wanted to know himself.

The streets were swarming. The strike had emptied workshops and factories, there were no street-cars running, and what traffic there was could scarcely get through. Some shops had been broken into. Old women were scuttling furtively away with bags of looted food half hidden under their shawls. Men were drinking vodka from the bottle. There was not a policeman in sight. They had all gone to ground. Wisely, Dave thought. These Russian cops were not much beloved by the ordinary citizens.

Many people, like himself, were just drifting around out of curiosity, standing on corners, waiting for what happened next. But there were big groups in constant, purposeful movement, surging down one street and into the next, like flocks of birds responsive to some mysterious impulse.

There were soldiers among them – and not a few of the civilians now carried arms. He saw some with rifles slung across their backs and revolvers bulging their pockets. There was a rumour that the Arsenal had been broken into and the weapons handed out to the workers. It was said that the Fortress of St Peter and St Paul had opened its gates to them, that they had stormed and sacked the Ochrana Headquarters.

Chaos had come to the city. No one seemed to be in

control. When he approached the Winter Palace he found that he could not pass. Loyal troops surrounded it, along with the Admiralty building next door. The Governor was somewhere inside, besieged in the heart of the city he could no longer govern.

But who governed the rest of Petersburg – if anybody? Dave turned away and followed a column of excited demonstrators, bellowing slogans and brandishing red flags. They led him along the riverfront, under the windows of the proud mansions that rose behind the Neva embankments, past the Trinity Bridge and the Alexander, to the white-columned Tauride Palace on the other side of the city.

This, he knew, was the meeting-house of the Duma, the nation's elected representatives, the men who had no say in the nation's affairs, the men the Tsar would not listen to. What could they do now? What could anyone expect them to do?

'They must take over the government,' an old man assured him, wagging his head emphatically. 'The Tsar's ministers have bolted like rabbits! Let the Duma take over. Glory to God I have lived to see this day!'

The courtyard of the Tauride was thronged with people, pressing up to the colonnade, clamouring for news, decisions, instructions. Nobody knew anything for certain. If this is a revolution, thought Dave, no one has made it, it has made itself.

Suddenly there was a cry at the front:

'Kerensky!'

It was taken up behind. 'Kerensky! Quiet! Kerensky will tell us something!'

A hush fell. Between two of the white pillars Dave saw a dark figure, hand dramatically upraised. This must be the famous Kerensky, that Anton had told him about, the firebrand of the Duma, the brilliant young lawyer who was also a Socialist Revolutionary.

He was pale and looked even paler, for he wore a sombre suit and a black blouse, like a workman's, buttoned at the neck. He spoke rapidly, in staccato phrases, jerking his cropped head for emphasis, sometimes narrowing his eyes almost to slits. Whether he said anything definite or practical, Dave could not follow well enough to be sure. But the man was certainly an inspired orator, and the crowd rose to him with something like hysteria.

'People call me a mad idealist,' he concluded, 'but thank God for the idealists in this world!'

While they all cheered and shouted, he went back inside the building, and there was no chance to ask questions.

Dave fell into conversation with a young corporal from the Pavlovsky Regiment. He found the Russians always interested in foreigners, and for his own part he seized every chance to practise the language.

'Oh, Kerensky's all right,' said the corporal. 'I haven't much use for the rest of the Duma – too many fine gentle-men in frock coats with eye-glasses. But Kerensky belongs to the Soviets as well – and the Soviets represent us ordinary chaps.'

'What *are* the Soviets?' Dave asked. Only in the past day or two had he even heard the word.

The corporal explained. A soviet was a committee. 'In our regiment we have just elected a soviet to speak for us. In the other units also. The factories, the warships, they are all electing such soviets. But we must have a centre, a leadership. So I think all the soviets are to join together and have a headquarters. They will tell the Duma what we want. They are more our own sort.'

Just then there was a disturbance at the back of the crowd. Some open trucks, festooned with red bunting and packed with men, were nosing their way yard by yard towards the Palace entrance. There was much cheering and waving.

'It's the prisoners,' said the corporal.

'What prisoners?'

'Oh, the politicals. All the jails have been opened, same as the police-stations.'

Dave did not stay to hear more. He had seen Anton grinning triumphantly over the side of the second truck. With a delighted cry of greeting he began to wriggle his way through the throng.

It was the same gawky Anton, with eyes blazing like torches in the sockets of a face that had always been pale and bony, even before his spell in prison. They had cropped his dark hair and his chin was bristly but otherwise he was unchanged.

He dropped from the high truck, slipped on the frozen snow, and ended up in Dave's arms, hugging him and stammering incoherently with joy.

'Anton! This is wonderful!' Dave managed to disentangle himself. 'Say, Madame will be crazy when she sees you! *And* Linda! We must get word to Sonya too – we've all been so worried about you.'

'There will be much to tell,' said Anton importantly.

'Come on, then! Let's get going. We'll be in time for dinner. I just want to see their faces when we walk in!'

Anton, however, took some persuading. He wanted to know what was happening at the Tauride Palace, he thought perhaps the rescued prisoners ought to stay together, someone might want to question them.

It took a little while to convince Anton that nobody was sure what was happening and that there was noone in authority to ask him questions. The only people interested in his story would be his friends at the Pension.

The thought of food, hot water and clean clothing finally persuaded Anton to drag himself away. He shook hands emotionally with all his late fellow-prisoners, vowed undying comradeship, and set off with Dave.

Dave could see he was weak with underfeeding and lack of exercise, so he did not set too fast a pace. He kept a hopeful eye open for a taxi or a droshky, but all traffic seemed to have vanished from the unswept streets. At rare intervals they saw a patrolling armoured car or a truck full of armed workmen with red armlets and cockades or a motor-cyclist roaring by with urgent dispatches. That was all. They had to walk. Anton was flagging when they turned down by the frozen canal and saw Yasha peering furtively from the doorway.

The janitor gaped at the sight of Anton, then shambled forward, all smiles, bowing.

Dave guessed it was an uncomfortable time for *dvorniks* and others who usually worked for the police. Their protectors had made themselves scarce. People who had been spied on and betrayed in the past had now a chance of revenge.

A similar thought occurred to Anton. As he slowly climbed the stairs, his arm stretched heavily along the banisters, he muttered suddenly:

'What about Zorin? Is he still here?'

'Yes—'

'You found the warning in my letter?'

'Sure.'

'A man I met in prison . . . he said that there was something strange about Zorin . . . that perhaps he was a policeman in disguise.'

'Zorin – a policeman? Sure, we thought you meant that. We investigated, Linda and I.' Dave laughed. 'You'll be surprised! Zorin's a secret Bolshevik!'

'Truly?' Anton's weary face lit up. 'But this is wonderful! I have learnt much while I have been away – I have talked to some very interesting people. We organized our own lectures and discussions in the prison. I have come to a conclusion: most likely the Bolshevik theory of revolution is correct.'

'You certainly haven't changed,' said Dave. 'You catch new theories like diseases – even when you're in jail!'

There was no chance to say more. They had reached the door of the Pension. A minute later they were in the midst of an uproarious welcome-home, with Madame waltzing round the dinner-table in Anton's arms, old Anya sobbing joyfully and glorying to God, Linda shooting off unheeded questions like a machine-gun, and Mr Zorin twinkling genially in the background.

And Mr Zorin, Dave noticed, had brightened his sombre businessman's suit with a necktie of revolutionary red.

Things happened quickly and confusedly during the next two or three days. Dave started a letter home, then laid it aside unfinished. Whatever he wrote would be out of date long before it arrived.

The whole garrison of St Petersburg was in mutiny. At

Kronstadt, the naval base nearby, the sailors had risen against their officers.

The Governor of St Petersburg had abandoned even the headquarters he had set up in the Admiralty: the rebels had given him twenty minutes to get out, or he would be bombarded by the guns of Peter-Paul fortress across the river.

The Tsar's ministers had fled from their offices. The Duma had set up a 'Provisional Government', a temporary arrangement to restore order in the city and keep things going until a government could be elected by democratic means.

Anton did not think much of the Provisional Government. It included a prince and a multi-millionaire: would such people lead the Russian masses to freedom and equality? Mr Zorin nodded approvingly. There was more hope, he agreed, in the Soviets, whose Executive Committee was now firmly established in one wing of the Tauride Palace – they might not have many clear-headed Bolsheviks among them, but at least they were genuine working-class men and their hearts were in the right place. Anton, who had never soiled his hands with anything but ink, agreed with this enthusiastically. Factory-workers, poor peasants, private soldiers . . . they were the ones who mattered.

Not for the first time, Dave thought to himself that Anton would never be the ideal friend to take home – if ever so unlikely an opportunity arose. Dad wouldn't exactly see eye to eye with Anton. Not till he switched to some new gospel, anyway.

Meanwhile, what was happening in the rest of the country? It was next to impossible to discover. What was the Tsar doing – if anything? What did the rest of the Army think of the garrison's behaviour?

Mr Zorin seemed to know more than most people. Dave got the feeling that Mr Zorin was no rank-and-file revolutionary but someone quite important in his party organization, maybe on committees where information could be picked up. The man had all the marks of a professional. He said little, he did not argue with people who didn't matter, like Miss Upton, he didn't rush around flaunting his opinions. The red tie was no more than a quiet indication of sympathy, an insurance against trouble with an excitable crowd. Otherwise, Mr Zorin went his way quietly and without fuss, though now he would sometimes talk politics with Anton and lend him books that he had previously kept hidden, books by people like Karl Marx, that would have been dangerous to leave about in the old days.

It was Mr Zorin who told them that the Tsar had ordered the Duma to disband, that he was sending a general with four regiments of front-line troops to recapture the capital ... For a day or two Dave wondered if Petersburg was going to be the scene of bombardment and street-fighting.

But no. The next news was that the railway workers were blocking all troop-movements within a hundred and fifty miles of the city. Nicholas himself could not get through: the imperial train was stranded at Pskov. At Tsarskoe Selo the garrison had mutinied: the Tsarina, her son and daughters, were marooned defenceless on their country estate.

'I cannot credit it,' sniffed Miss Upton. 'Rumours! Propaganda! No one would dare. They would have more respect.'

What a week it had been! It was on Monday that the Petersburg soldiers had come out on the side of the people and that Anton had escaped from his ten-weeks imprisonment. It was only Friday now . . .

Sonya had telephoned. She had not been able to get leave before – in the Ballet School, if nowhere else, the old discipline was preserved – but she was to be free after her classes, she could come for the evening she wanted to see Anton and hear about his adventures.

The city was quieter now. There were no more smouldering police-stations, no drunken looters capering round the vodka-shops, no trigger-happy Red Guards. All the same, Madame Mitrova said it would be better if Anton and Dave went to fetch her.

Fresh snow was falling, soft, woolly, soundless. When they reached the School they found a crowd of people on the whitening pavement, staring upwards. Looking up, eyes narrowed against the flakes, they saw dark figures perched round the top of a ladder, straining at some task high above the portico.

'Stand back!' bellowed a deep voice from the gloom overhead. The spectators obediently scattered. 'Here we go, citizens!'

There was a raucous cheer as something massive hurtled through the air, hit the flagstones with a crash, and sent dust and splinters flying in every direction.

Then, as the workmen came nimbly down the ladder, the crowd surged forward. Someone stooped, picked up a fragment, and brandished it with a laugh of mockery. In the light streaming from the School doorway Dave saw what it was. It was two eagle-heads, joined at the neck, the emblem of imperial majesty.

Dave turned and saw Sonya greeting Anton. The tears were streaming down her cheeks. She swung round.

'David! Is it true?'

'What?' he asked puzzled.

'What these men have been shouting. They say that the Tsar has given up his throne – they say we haven't an emperor any more!'

CHAPTER FOURTEEN

Lunch with the Ambassador

A new flag flew over the Winter Palace, blood-red against the leaden sky.

What Sonya had heard was true. Nicholas II had faced the hard truth: almost his whole people, high and low, were against him. He had agreed to step down from the throne of the Romanovs. He had asked his doctor if there was any hope that his son would grow up healthy. Being assured that the boy's disease was incurable, he had seen no point in passing on to him the burden of an unhappy crown. He had proposed his own younger brother, the Grand Duke Michael, as the next tsar. Michael, sensing the nation's mood, had refused the honour, unless it were offered to him by a democratic assembly. So, as Sonya said, there was no longer an emperor in Russia. And, to judge from the flowering of red flags everywhere, like poppies in a cornfield, and the disappearance of the eagles and other imperial insignia, it looked as if there would never be one again.

At the Pension Yalta there was an electric atmosphere.

Anya went about her work like one stunned. She muttered and crossed herself at frequent intervals. To her, the fall of the Little Father was akin to the end of the world. Who knew? Perhaps the end of the world *would* be the next blow?

The effect on Miss Upton was no less severe, though she displayed more self-control. 'Very well,' she said with majestic disapproval, 'I have finished with Russia. As soon as the state of the war permits, I shall ask the British Consul if it is not possible for me to travel. St Petersburg is no place for me now. I shall be happier with my sister in England. Malvern may not be St Petersburg,' she said generously. 'It lacks the river. But then St Petersburg has not the hills. Yes, Malvern will suit me better now.'

Even the stolid Mr Zorin seemed shaken by the rapid developments of the past week.

'It is not what I expected,' he admitted. 'We must all learn to adjust ourselves. Whatever turn things take, there is always a way of exploiting it to advantage.' He wasted three precious matches before he could get his pipe going. A full week passed before he was known to write another letter.

Between Anton and Sonya there was bitter war. Dave had never heard the girl so eloquent. Over and over again she declared that Anton's wild friends would ruin Russia.

'Nonsense!' reported the student. 'Russia will be transformed – set free—'

'Tell me how!'

'When I do, you will not listen!'

'Oh, politics!' She stamped her foot. 'Socialism!'

'Children!' pleaded Madame. Dave and Linda could only look on and listen, following the argument as best they could with their imperfect Russian, but powerless to stop it.

'You are a dreamer!' Sonya declared.

'And you are asleep,' said Anton, 'but you do not even dream! The world rushes by, you hear nothing, you do not understand, you are an *artist*,' he concluded with heavy scorn.

'Better an artist than a savage!'

'Are you calling me a savage?'

'Your Bolshevik friends, anyhow. They invade Kshesinskaya's beautiful home, with its priceless art treasures – they turn it into their headquarters—'

'Aha! Now we are coming to the really grave issue, the unforgivable outrage!' Anton turned to the others, breaking into English. 'It is not the fall of the Tsar that shocks our little Sonya! It is for our famous ballerina that she is really concerned.'

He explained, with furious interruptions from Sonya, that Kshesinskaya had been one of the great dancers of the previous generation. She had a mansion beside the Neva, a fantastic over-decorated building like an Oriental pagoda, furnished with gifts lavished on her in bygone days by the Tsar and his nobles. It was quite true: the Bolsheviks had established their offices in the house – but they had merely taken it over from a regimental club that had been using it since the war began.

'It is no worse than your hospital using a Grand Duke's palace,' he said, appealing to Linda. 'As for the works of art, they will not be harmed, they will be covered up and kept out of the way—'

'How do you know?' Sonya demanded.

'Because it is policy, idiot! It is all written in the paper – I have it somewhere—' Anton fumbled through his pockets and after some delay produced a page torn from *New Life*. Spreading out the crumpled sheet of newsprint he declaimed:

' *"Citizens! The old masters have departed and a vast inheritance remains. Today it is the property of the whole*

*people. Citizens, take care of this inheritance, take care of
the palaces, the pictures, the statues—" '*

'All right, all right! Who says that?'

'The greatest living writer in Russia,' said Anton triumphantly. 'Maxim Gorki! You call yourself an artist –
Gorki speaks for the artists, and he backs the Revolution!'

'Oh, you have an answer to everything.' Sonya flung
out of the room in tears. 'I cannot argue with you.'

Dave and Linda looked at each other helplessly. Who
was right? It was all so complicated, and in this quarrel
between their friends they did not want to take sides.

One thing that helped Dave to make up his mind was an
invitation – well, it was a summons really, he guessed – to
take lunch with no less a person than the United States
Ambassador. Mr Francis (explained young Mr Hayes over
the telephone) had promised Dave's father to keep an eye
on him.

Dave made a face as he hung up the receiver. At least,
he consoled himself, he would get a good lunch. Mr
Francis did not go in for a lot of stuffy dinner-parties but
his taste in food was legendary. He had shaken Dave's
hand and spoken a kindly word at the Christmas party,
but beyond that he was a stranger, though Dave knew him
well by sight – he was not a man you could miss in winter-
time anyhow, for he drove around the city in a horse-
drawn sleigh with American flags attached to the bridles,
rather to the amusement of the more conventional
diplomats.

The American Embassy was on the eastern side of the
city, a long way from the Winter Palace but quite near to

the Tauride, where the Provisional Government was established.

There was something appropriate about this, Dave soon realized, for Mr Francis, an elderly businessman from Missouri, seemed a lot closer in sympathy with the new leaders and their democratic hopes than with the old Tsarist order.

There were no other guests. The Ambassador, he said, wanted a quiet chat, the way they'd have had it back home, without any frills. After the meal, they moved to easy chairs, and Mr Francis lit a cigar. He kept a large spittoon beside his right foot. It had a lid which came up as he pressed the pedal. Their chat was punctuated by occasional clicks and clanks as he made use of this handy apparatus.

'Well, son,' he said, after a few questions about Dave's life in St Petersburg, 'I guess your Dad's been getting worried this past week or two – leastways, your Mom has.'

'That's more likely, sir,' said Dave with a smile.

'They sent me a telegram, a long telegram. Seems this revolution has scared your Mom. Want to know if you shouldn't be getting out o' here.'

'Oh, *no*, sir!' Dave's smile faded.

'You don't want to go?' The Ambassador removed the cigar from his lips. Click, went the spittoon. Clank, the lid fell back into place. 'It's up to you, son. Course, anything can happen in this country. But *I* wouldn't say this was the time to quit.'

'No, sir.'

'Things have gotten into a bad state, but I reckon the tide has turned. This new government looks hopeful to me. And to the President in Washington. He's talking about "the wonderful and heartening things happening in Russia". That's my own estimate. Give this new set-up a chance to get things organized and we'll see some progress. Russia will be right back in the war, helping to lick the Germans.'

They talked for a little while longer. Dave was interested, and rather surprised, to hear how the revolution appeared to someone who was a businessman like his father but knew so much more about it at close quarters. 'Well, as I say,' Mr Francis concluded, 'if you or your folks requested it, I could fix you a passage home. But I don't think it's necessary – and I don't think it's advisable at this time.'

Something in his tone, as he spoke the last words, caught Dave's special notice. ' "Advisable", sir?' he echoed. 'Surely it would be *safe* – as a neutral?'

'You might not always be a neutral,' said Mr Francis dryly. His face gave nothing away. He was not only a diplomat and a businessman, he was a keen poker-player too. A boy like Dave was not going to get any more out of him than he meant to reveal.

A secretary came in and whispered in his ear. Mr Francis stood up and held out his hand. 'It's been fine meeting you, son. Got to go, now. Some urgent telegrams, they're just decoding them.' There was a light in his shrewd eyes. 'A busy time. Going to be busier, I guess. I'll send a word to your folks, though. No cause to worry.'

Dave went home much relieved. More than ever, he was set on remaining in Russia.

Next day, he was able to make a good guess at the urgent telegrams that had called the Ambassador away. The newspapers came out with exultant headlines. President Wilson had declared war on Germany. America's millions – her dollars, her men and her munitions – were thrown into the scale against the enemy. Victory was certain now.

Linda was so carried away by the news that she flung her arms round Dave and kissed him. 'That's because we're allies at last!' she explained breathlessly.

Dave was sorry Sonya wasn't there. America wasn't only Britain's ally now, she was Russia's too.

CHAPTER FIFTEEN

The Man from Switzerland

Anton, to Dave's disappointment, showed no enthusiasm for America's action. But then Anton had no enthusiasm for the war.

In prison his quicksilver mind had come under new influences. A man who had shared his cell had converted him to the teachings of Karl Marx. War, he was now convinced, was the fault of the rich, the capitalist, the imperialist. German or Russian, British or French or American, the upper classes were all tarred with the same brush, and there was nothing to choose between them. They lived only for profit, grinding the faces of the poor, and wars were fought solely for their interests. The common people must unite all over the world, overthrow their governments and the wicked capitalist system, and establish communism. Then there would be peace and plenty everywhere.

' "Working men of all countries, unite!" ' Anton declaimed the quotation – he was very fond of quotations nowadays. ' "You have nothing to lose but your chains: you have a world to win!" '

Dave still thought it might be a good idea to start by winning the war. If the Germans went on advancing into Russia and reached St Petersburg where would Anton and his new Bolshevik friends be?

But it was little use to argue with Anton. He knew it all, and believed it fervently, until he read something fresh and was smitten by another idea. For the present he seemed firmly rooted in his latest creed. He was mixing with Bolsheviks every day. Though they had not yet accepted him as a member of their party (they seemed strangely choosy, thought Dave, considering how badly they needed support), they gave him work in the offices of their newspaper *Pravda*, which they were now allowed to publish again for the first time since the war began. Anton's command of English was valuable. He was kept busy translating items from the British and American press.

For the moment, though, the Bolshevik view of the war was not popular. There was a new spirit in the Army. Whereas before the soldiers had been deserting in droves, they now took fresh heart and resolved to fight on. If they let the Germans walk over them, the Kaiser would rescue the Tsar and set him on the throne again. Weren't the two emperors cousins, even though their countries were at war?

King George of England was another cousin, come to that . . . Linda heard that the King had offered the Tsar a refuge in England. Miss Upton was at first delighted, then furious when she learnt that the Provisional Government had finally decided not to let him go.

'Even the Provisional Government are not such idiots!' said Anton in his lordly way. 'If the Tsar escapes abroad, he will start a counter-revolution to win back his throne. He is better where he is.'

So the Tsar stayed with his family on their country estate, under close guard. He must not leave Russia. Nor must he fall into the hands of the Germans. Nor could he go free.

'There is no need for you to worry about me,' Dave

wrote home. *'Things are getting back to normal here, except that all the eagles and the Tsar's portraits and so forth are pulled down, and we have red flags everywhere instead. The street-cars are running again and people are back at work and the soldiers are obeying orders, though there isn't so much saluting – they all reckon themselves as good as the officers, when they are off duty, which I don't think some of the officers like very much, only I guess they daren't say so. There is a new City Governor, General Kornilov, who is a Cossack but seems to be trusted by the new government – this is interesting, because ordinary Russians don't much care for the Cossacks; they're like a people apart, and in the past the Tsars have always used them to break up meetings and such like, often very brutally. They use horrible whips, called "knouts". Still, this Kornilov seems okay, and he has certainly restored order in the garrison . . . It's April here now, even by their calendar, but not much sign of spring yet as I guess there will be with you. They say the river thaws out late in April. It's the Russian Easter next week, with picturesque ceremonies and customs. Should be interesting . . .'*

Dave was looking forward to Easter even more than he revealed in his letter.

'But naturally Sonya will come home!' said Madame. 'Easter is our great festival. We Russians feel deeply. In Holy Week all is sadness and gloom. There is no place even for the ballet. Afterwards, though, we are rejoicing, because of the Resurrection. You will see.'

Anton snorted. Religion, he quoted, was 'the opium of the people'. He refused to escort the ladies to Midnight Mass on the Saturday. Dave did not mind. Now it would have to be Sonya who stood beside him in the dark cathedral and explained in whispers what was happening.

It was a strange service, almost more like a play, or perhaps an opera, because the singing and chanting of these deep Russian voices produced an effect he was always to remember. Then it was as though the bearded bishop was acting the drama of the first Easter morning.

'See,' Sonya murmured huskily. 'He goes to the Holy Sepulchre . . . and now he raises the cloth . . . that is for the shroud . . . he shows that there is no body – the tomb is empty—'

Now the mime was carried a stage further. The bishop and the other clergy and the choristers went out of the church in procession. No one else moved. Dave whispered:

'Is it over?'

'No, no! They must walk all round the church outside – they act that they are searching for Our Lord's body. When they do not find it, they know for certain that He has risen from the dead.'

Dave felt the tension in the congregation round him. It was extraordinary. It was just an ancient ritual, he told himself – he could understand why Anton called it childish play-acting, though he couldn't go along with Anton in all his opinions – but to these people, wrought up in their emotions, it was as though it was really happening. They were waiting. Even Sonya beside him was keyed up.

Those few minutes seemed an age. Then the procession came back, moving slowly forward over the flagstones. The bishop turned and faced the congregation, his face transfigured with joy. He let out a triumphant cry.

'Christ is risen!'

And, like a cheering army, the people roared back:

'In truth, He is risen!'

Magically, lighted tapers appeared and were handed round. Everyone had to hold a taper. They twinkled through the church like glow-worms. They gleamed on the gold and silver ikons, the splendidly coloured Byzantine mosaics, now suddenly revealed after being covered throughout Holy Week.

'And now,' Sonya whispered shyly, almost apologetically, 'I must kiss you – it is the Easter kiss of peace and brotherly love.'

Solemnly she kissed him three times, and then she turned to her grandmother and Linda and Miss Upton, and did the same, and Dave had to follow suit because it was obviously part of the service and the whole congregation was doing it.

There was more singing, but happy singing now, thunderous and exultant. Then they all went out into the midnight streets, and walked home, and he had Linda on one arm and Sonya on the other, with all the bells of St Petersburg pealing together in crazy joy.

Of course, it wasn't like the wonderful peacetime Easters Miss Upton remembered with her princely families, when there had been tremendous banquet-like suppers following the Midnight Mass, scores of liveried retainers lining up to offer their greetings and receive their gifts, and a marvellous display of Easter eggs.

Madame and Anya had done their best. Somehow they had managed to buy enough ordinary eggs for each member of the family. The eggs were hard boiled, each wrapped in a different scrap of coloured cloth, so that the dye came off on the shell. For everyone there was a *kulich*, a special kind of roll eaten only at this season, and a cheese-cake called *pashka*. And Sonya had made paper roses to decorate the ikon.

'Childish superstitions,' muttered Anton, but he did not refuse the *kulich* and *pashka* offered him, or the scarlet-dyed egg which Madame carefully selected for him, with a teasing smile, from the multi-coloured assortment in the dish.

All too soon the festival was over. Sonya returned to school, the glow died, life resumed its 1917 greyness.

On the day after Easter Anton hurried back from the newspaper office. 'You want to see something?' he asked Dave excitedly. 'Come, get your cap and coat—'

'Where are we going?'

'To the Finland Station!'

'And then where?' Dave was always amused by Anton's impulsiveness.

The student blinked at the question. 'Nowhere! We are not catching a train – we are meeting one.'

Dave stood up, not sorry to have an excuse to close his Russian textbook. 'Why?' he inquired good-naturedly.

'I have just heard. Lenin is arriving!'

'Lenin? Oh, you mean that guy you're always talking about? The one who's been in exile all these years?'

'The Bolshevik.' Anton nodded vigorously. 'He has the keenest mind of them all – I have read his articles – he explains how to fit the ideas of Karl Marx to our present situation in Russia—'

'You told me,' Dave interrupted hastily. 'But I thought he was in Switzerland or some place.'

'He was.'

'Then how come he's on a train arriving at the Finland Station? You only arrive there from Scandinavia. *I* should know.'

'There is some mystery. They think at the office that the Germans let him through – from Switzerland across to

Sweden, that is.' Anton was dancing with impatience. 'What does it matter? So long as he gets here? We need his leadership, his genius for organizing. Are you coming or not?'

'Okay, okay. If this guy's half as wonderful as you make out, he must be worth seeing. I guess this country can always use a bit more organization.'

'We must hurry then, if we wish to get a good view. We shall not be the only ones waiting at the station.'

That was a notable understatement.

'*The crowds were making that way,*' Dave recorded in his next letter, '*like it was a ball game back home.*'

They found the square in front of the Finland Station a heaving mass of spectators. The spring afternoon was over. It was almost dark. A searchlight mounted on an armoured car cut golden swathes around the square, picking out the pallid faces, the red flags, the banners and slogans. It looked as though the whole city was waiting for Lenin.

'They sure think a lot of him,' Dave murmured. He was privately mystified. The man had been out of Russia for years. He was only a name to these people, after all – a faked name at that, most likely, for most of these revolutionaries had had to cover up their tracks in days gone by. He might be a big noise among the Bolsheviks, but they were only one section among many. They must have passed the word round very effectively, to gather a welcome-home committee this size.

'Here we shall see nothing,' said Anton. 'I shall try to get us admission to the station.'

'You got a hope!' said Dave. But a minute or two later he was saying admiringly, 'You got a nerve!' For Anton, normally so impractical, could be quite ingenious when his enthusiasm drove him on.

Waving his identity card, continually repeating that he was on the staff of *Pravda* and that Dave represented the American press, he ploughed a way for them to the side entrance. A company of soldiers was drawn up there. For a moment Dave wondered if they had been sent to break up the crowd. But Anton explained with some indignation. This was the door by which Lenin would leave. The soldiers were a guard of honour. Dave thought that decidedly curious. After all, this guy was just a private person, he wasn't in this new government, in fact by all accounts he didn't even support it, he was really nobody . . .

Dave's amazement grew when they got inside the station. It was decorated with flags and triumphal arches all along the platform. They might have been expecting an emperor. In fact, they had opened up the old imperial waiting room – it was bright with lights and full of solemn-looking politicians and trade union men whispering together. Someone actually had a bouquet ready. In this country it was okay, it seemed, to give men flowers. And there was an army band where Lenin's coach was scheduled to pull in.

Dave remembered his own arrival six months earlier and grinned. 'I guess you didn't lay on this treatment for me,' he whispered. But Anton was too absorbed in the scene to respond to any light-hearted comments.

They had a long wait. At last the train was signalled, the band sprang to attention and raised their instruments, the glass doors of the Tsar's waiting room opened and the reception committee streamed out. Excitedly Anton identified the leaders he knew by sight.

'That is our new editor, Kamenev. Behind him is the previous editor, Molotov. The fellow with Kamenev is a Georgian – his name is Stalin – they both came back from exile in Siberia a month ago—' Anton stopped, open-mouthed, dumb.

'*Zorin!*' hissed Dave.

There was no doubt of it. They had both recognized him in the same instant as he came out on to the platform. For once he was not puffing at his pipe, but in every other respect it was their own unmistakable Mr Zorin. Quiet, genial but modest and self-effacing, he trailed out behind the notables. Dave's hunch had been right. Zorin was no rank-and-file Bolshevik. He was one of the big men.

The train glided in. The tall locomotive crept towards them like a hissing cat, drawing in (like a tongue) the last yards of glistening track. Brassy, strident under the station roof, the band struck up the *Marseillaise*.

'There he is!' said Anton. 'That must be him! In the cap – with the beard! Yes, they have given him the flowers! Yes, that is Lenin!'

Dave never dared to admit it to Anton, but at first he was disappointed, after all that fuss and expectancy, to see such an ordinary figure. Lenin was small and stocky, he had a snub nose and almost piggy eyes, his clothes were shabby and shapeless. He looked like any other insignificant traveller, chilled and weary from a long second-class journey. So this was the much-awaited man from Switzerland? It was incongruous to see him ushered so respectfully into that imperial waiting-room, as though he had replaced the Tsar as ruler of Russia.

A quarter of an hour later, Dave began to wonder if he hadn't better revise his judgment.

The private welcomes over, he had seen Lenin pass quickly out of the station and heard the roar of the tens of thousands massed outside. Surely there must be something about a man who could command a reception like this?

The searchlight, slanting down from the roof of an armoured car, picked up that bearded face, held it as though in the theatre, followed it as Lenin made his way to another armoured car and clambered up to use it as a platform. A hush fell. All eyes were fixed on that small grey figure, that mere manikin in its ring of yellow light, dwarfed by the vastness of its surroundings. All ears strained to catch the words.

'Dear comrades, soldiers, sailors, workers—'

The multitude roared back in joyful approval.

Dave could not follow all the speech. But he understood the thunderous climax and the applause that greeted it.

'*Long live the world revolution!*'

The armoured car began to creep forward through the crowd. The searchlight still held it, still held the man from Switzerland as he rode aloft, like some modern cloth-capped Caesar entering his capital in triumph. Other armoured cars, other vehicles, nosed their way into an informal procession behind. The crowd pressed after them, out of the square and into the narrower streets beyond.

The boys followed until they lost sight of the figure spot-lit on its moving pedestal of steel. Then Anton turned to Dave and tossed off one of those flamboyant phrases he loved.

'Yesterday, my friend, you looked at Russia's past: tonight you have looked upon her future!'

CHAPTER SIXTEEN

The White Nights

Now, in a warm rush, came the northern spring.

The snow-heaps melted into dirty water and fled gurgling down the gutters. The ice on canal and river groaned and cracked across. The jagged floes raced away to the Gulf of Finland, bobbing and tilting and turning over in the current. Every morning there seemed to be less ice and more water, and the water itself was losing its milky greyness, until soon it was blue under the cloudless sky and sparkling in the sunshine, that same sunshine that washed golden over the palaces and public buildings, until Dave could see why Peter the Great had brought Italian architects to design his cold new capital. On such days it no longer seemed so crazy to imitate the cities of the South.

May brought out all the leaves, the first flowers. In no time the spring had merged into the short, hot Russian summer. The very days lengthened like the green shoots, almost as you watched. Every evening the sun went down later and later into the shimmering Gulf. The White Nights were coming: by midsummer the last pale glow of one day would linger in the sky almost until it merged into the dawn of the next.

In such weather everyone sighed for the country.

'When I was with the Princess,' Miss Upton recalled

mistily, 'we had such picnics, such carriage-drives through the woods . . .'

Madame, in her more prosperous days, had owned a *datcha* or country cottage twenty miles from Petersburg, but those lazy summer holidays belonged (like Miss Upton's memories) to another epoch. She had the Pension to run, and the mere finding of food for each meal was a whole-time task. That summer the prices soared to seven times what they had been before the war.

Sonya was the lucky one. The Ballet School had an old wooden house on the Kamenny Ostrov, one of the remoter, more northerly islands that, like pieces of a jigsaw puzzle, composed the pattern of the city. At this time of the year the senior pupils were moved out there to enjoy the sunshine and the sea air. They had only to cross a near-by bridge to find themselves on the last island of all, the Yelagin Ostrov, unspoilt and park-like, with shady walks ending in a sudden view-point, a little promontory thrust out into the open sea.

'Oh, in the old days it was wonderful, wonderful,' said Miss Upton. 'I can't tell you!' But she proceeded to do so. 'The smart carriages, the coachmen, the officers in their white summer uniforms, the ladies with their parasols – all the world drove out to Yelagin to see the sunset over the Gulf. Imagine, Linda my dear, the elegance of a London season but with something added! Hyde Park, one might say, beside the sea.'

Those glories had faded. The glossy carriages were laid up, the horses had gone to the war, the pavilions and boat-houses were shuttered. Instead of yachts skimming to and fro like butterflies there were only grey submarines and mine-sweepers and tall-funnelled cruisers anchored in the offing.

None the less, Sonya clearly loved her summer on the island.

The girls were allowed to take walks, but only in pairs. Dave slyly found out the usual time and quite soon after Sonya's move he managed, by a not very convincing coincidence, to be walking across the Yelagin bridge just as she appeared with her friend Vera. Sonya introduced him, and, after a cautious backward glance towards the house they had left, agreed that he might escort them to the westerly tip of the island.

They walked slowly, sometimes through shady alleys that plunged them into a muted green light as though they were under the sea, at other times in the full blaze of the sunshine, with glassy wavelets slapping the edge of the path.

Vera was as vivacious as Sonya was quiet and thoughtful. She was a blue-eyed, corn-haired girl from Kiev in the Ukraine. She knew no English, but Dave could now carry on a fluent conversation, and there were no awkward silences. Laughter, anyhow, is an international language. There was plenty of that.

They took leave of him at a prudent distance from the School hostel, gravely shaking hands.

'Perhaps another day—' he suggested.

'It would be nice if you could persuade Anton to come,' said Sonya.

'I'll try. But you know what he is. He spends most of his time on this translating for *Pravda*.'

'I know. All the same,' she added firmly, 'four is a better number.'

Sure, he told himself as he walked away. He thought he knew what she meant. He hoped he did. But he couldn't see Anton having much in common with a frivolous chat-terbox like Vera.

He was right.

Anton was much too wrapped up in his new work and talked airily of taking up journalism as a career – though this was no moment, he remarked, with a dig at Sonya in her absence, for anyone to be thinking of personal careers. History was being made, not only Russia's but the world's.

Madame would catch Dave's eye and smile reassuringly when Anton talked of his work.

'It is good for the boy to be occupied,' she murmured privately. 'In any case the University has dispersed for the summer – and who knows if he will be taken back next term after he has been in prison? Much will depend on who is then in power. Again, who knows?'

Who knew, indeed?

The Provisional Government was not producing any miracles. Conditions in Petersburg seemed no better than they had been before the February revolution. Prices were higher, food shorter. Factories closed. More and more workers were laid off. Important delegations arrived in the city from the Allied countries; American, British, French, demanding that Russia should pull herself together and make a final push to topple the Germans and Austrians on the eastern front.

Dave's father wrote, irritably: *'What's gotten into your Russki friends? We are offering them a credit of one hundred million dollars to set them on their feet again. But they got to stay in the fight till the Germans are licked. No fight, no loan.'*

When Dave mentioned this to Mr Zorin he answered cynically:

'But of course! Your country prefers to spend the dollars while Russia spends the blood.'

'That's not fair, sir!' For once Dave was really angry. 'My father says we're raising a big army, but it's got to be trained and armed and shipped across the Atlantic. It can't be done in five minutes. All we're asking is that you should hang on and hold the fort a bit longer, the way the French and British are doing. Then victory is certain.'

'We are not interested in that kind of victory,' said Anton, joining the argument. 'The victory of nations does not concern the toiling masses. The only victory we care for is to overthrow the system that makes the wars and keeps the workers in poverty. Let Russia be beaten. It may be a good thing. It will make it easier for us to destroy the system and build again.'

'If anyone talked that way in our country, we'd say he was a traitor! Pro-German!'

'I am not pro-German, Dave. As for being a traitor, it depends on the point of view.'

'Well, I'm glad most Russians have a different point of view!'

Dave felt some confidence as he said that. For it was obvious that the Bolsheviks were still in the minority. The return of Lenin had made an impressive show, but it had led to nothing, so far as he could see. If anything, the Bolsheviks had lost some ground in popularity. Most people backed the Provisional Government, for all its faults. It was whispered that Lenin was a German spy. Without German help he could never have returned from exile.

'It makes me smile,' said Anton. 'What about the other leaders? What about Trotsky? *He* was in New York. Is he then an American spy? Because he could never have reached Petersburg without the help of you Americans?'

Whatever Lenin and Trotsky might say, the Government seemed resolved to carry on the war to victory. Linda said that a big offensive would be launched early in July.

'How do you know?' Dave demanded.

'Ah! In hospitals we know these things in advance.'

Kornilov, the Cossack general, had already resigned the governorship of the city and taken up a new command at the front. Some said he was disgusted because the Government would not let him use tough enough measures against the Bolsheviks; but maybe, thought Dave, it was because he was a fighting soldier and he did not want to miss the final battles with Germany.

June passed. St Petersburg took on the full loveliness of midsummer.

Dave walked for miles on those endless evenings. Now and again Anton walked with him: they might argue about the war and suchlike things, but that did not prevent their being friends. Anton was always fun to be with, always full of ideas. He might be crazy, Dave decided, but he was sincere.

Sometimes Linda was off duty and not too tired, so she went with them, or with Dave alone. They walked the granite embankments along the great river. They strolled in the public gardens or along the Nevsky. They explored the quieter canals, girdling the centre of the capital. When they had time, they took a street-car out to Kamenny Ostrov. Then they sauntered past the Ballet School hostel, hoping for a glimpse of Sonya, listening to the tinkle of a piano through an open window. When they could no longer lurk outside the house they would go on to Yelagin for the famous sunset, returning after midnight in a strange soft twilight like mother-of-pearl, neither darkness nor day, the legendary white night of the northern capital.

When he went by himself, Dave could stay even later. He was his own master. Unlike Anton and Linda, who had long spells of duty. He would stay out on the little promontory until the sunset was only a pale golden blur where sky and sea joined. He would stroll back very slowly under the murmurous trees. By the time he reached Kamenny Ostrov the Ballet School hostel would be dark and silent. The street-cars had stopped running. He had to walk every yard of the way back to the Pension. Once the dawn was coming up as he trudged across the Trinity Bridge. Yet he never felt really tired. There was an exhilaration in the sea air and the tree-scents breathing across the islands. There was a magic in the light, golden and silver, bright and soft. He would never forget that summer, he knew.

Yasha gave him some odd looks when he had to let him in.

'Do you think he still reports to the police?' Dave asked Anton.

'Who knows?' said Anton darkly. 'A true revolution would have abolished the Secret Police – but I can believe it still flourishes just as it did under the Tsar. But *you* need not worry about Yasha. By now he knows that you are non-political. He probably thinks you are carrying on a secret love-affair!' He laughed. Dave flushed and turned away. 'Give him a rouble or two for being wakened so early,' Anton advised, 'then he will take no further interest in your exits and entrances!'

Only once was Dave able to get Anton's company for an afternoon, so that they could catch Sonya and her friend on their walk. The girls seemed delighted to see them, and there was much laughter and chatter, but the expedition did not work out entirely as planned. Anton quickly summed up the other girl. 'Pretty enough, but politically an imbecile,' he told Dave afterwards. So, when the shady path grew narrower, it was Dave who found himself paired with Vera.

'Sonya is better,' said Anton generously, as the two boys stood in the jolting street-car, riding home. 'She is developing sense, that girl. She could be educated, given time.'

He could not see Dave's scowl, for they were pressed shoulder to shoulder in the sweating crowd of straphangers. Silly fool, thought Dave. He kids himself she agrees with him, just because she doesn't say much. I bet she wasn't listening to a word he said.

July brought good news from the front.

Linda's advance information had been correct: the Russian armies had launched an offensive. They had started in the south, where they faced the Austrians, the easier enemy. But soon, obviously, like a train of gun-powder, the fighting would flare all along the line, till they were driving back the Germans as well.

Miss Upton cheered up. Once more she stuck paper flags all over her wall-map. She still used the old imperial flag to represent the Russian troops. She had no red ones and refused to make them. She began to persuade herself that the Revolution was just a phase that would pass and could be ignored. The Tsar – she would always call him the Tsar – was still safe on his estate. 'Mark my words,' prophesied Miss Upton, 'when this nonsense is over, we shall see him back on his throne.'

'Poor old thing,' said Anton under his breath. 'Without doubt, she is going gaga.'

There must have been others who shared Miss Upton's hopes, but if they were sensible they kept quiet. In Petersburg the argument was between those who supported the Provisional Government, and wanted to bring the war to a victorious finish, and those who favoured the Bolshevik line, peace at once on almost any terms, and an end to the killing and the famine.

Now that Dave had been in the country long enough to have some idea of what the people had suffered in three years of war, he could not blame those who, like Anton, were swept away by the eloquent persuasion of the Bolsheviks.

They were so *certain*, these men, Lenin especially, hammering home their points with merciless logic. They knew what they wanted, when all the other parties seemed muddled and woolly-minded. They wanted power, and they were determined to get it.

They were not particular about methods. Dave saw that Anton was sometimes troubled by things that happened at the *Pravda* office. By the way, for instance, that his own translations from the foreign press were cut so that in the end a misleading impression was given to the Russian reader. He did his best to explain and justify this treatment, but Dave could tell that he was not happy.

'Of course,' said Anton, 'it happens in all newspapers. There must be sub-editing. If I make it too long, naturally they must cut. And mistakes occur. A journalist works at great speed.'

'Sure. But some of the pieces you've shown me – those changes aren't accidental. They've twisted the truth.'

'There is no absolute truth. All truth is relative.' It was

like a parrot's voice, Dave thought gloomily, repeating other people. Anton wouldn't have said that a few months ago. He used to talk about truth as something sacred. Was *he* being slowly and subtly twisted like his own translations?

'I'll argue that another time,' he said. 'But I guess some of these Bolshevik guys are mighty slick operators.'

'They need to be, with the odds so heavy against them. The end justifies the means. I heard Lenin say, last week, when he came into our office: "Revolution is a dirty job, you do not make it with white gloves." I do not like it, but I am learning that it is true.'

There was a thundery tension in Petersburg during those July days, both in the actual weather and in the mood of the people.

Wild rumours circulated, accusations were bandied about, the various parties screamed at each other in their newspapers and leaflets. Inside the government there were disputes and several ministers resigned. Some said the government itself was about to fall, others that the Bolsheviks were plotting an armed rising to overthrow it, others again that there was a devilish German plot to stab Russia in the back as her armies swept to victory at the front.

Dave did not try to explain to his father. He had only a muddled notion of what was happening. He went to a great number of public meetings, because listening to orators seemed an excellent way to improve his Russian. He heard most of the Government leaders, especially the magnetic spell-binder Kerensky, now Minister for War. He heard their Bolshevik critics – Lenin, cold, heavy, ferociously logical, and Trotsky, with his rich, deep voice, and many more. But he found these interminable debates beyond his understanding.

In mid-July there was violence again.

Thousands of mutinous sailors from Kronstadt came sailing into the river in destroyers and other small craft. They swarmed ashore, mingling with strikers in the centre of the city. There were riots. The soldiers wavered, some units loyal to the Provisional Government, some favouring the Bolsheviks. There was shooting, men were killed.

Yet, through all this, ordinary life went on. Anya did her marketing, Dave and Linda enjoyed an American movie, Anton worked early and late at the *Pravda* offices, Sonya practised to the endless thump and tinkle of the piano on her summer island . . .

'Life must go on,' said Madame, serenely ladling out the beetroot soup.

Dave still took his favourite walk to the seaward tip of Yelagin. He carried his books, but could not settle to study them. Sometimes he managed to contrive a seemingly accidental encounter with Sonya and Vera as they paraded sedately along the leafy avenues, but he did not dare to do it too often. Sonya, normally so quiet and controlled, became flustered and ill at ease. She was, he guessed, scared that they would be seen by one of the teachers. Nor did he himself find it satisfactory, with the voluble Vera always making a third.

The White Nights were passing, the interval between sunset and sunrise lengthening every time. Soon it would be getting fully dark again.

One afternoon, gazing out across the Gulf, Sonya

unwittingly gave him the cue he wanted. 'Fancy,' she said, 'I have never seen the midnight sunset here!'

Vera had moved some yards away, stepping gingerly over the rocks. For once Dave had a brief chance to speak to Sonya alone.

'Surely,' he said, 'you could slip out one evening? You're not a prisoner—'

'No, no, but—' Sonya seemed already frightened by what she had said.

'And you're not a child!' he pressed her.

For a minute or two they argued in low voices. Sonya had to admit it was possible. Other girls had been known . . . there was a ladder in the garden . . .

'I guess there's *always* a ladder,' said Dave, 'if folks set their minds on finding it.'

It took another two minutes to win her over. She denied that she was frightened, she could *not* deny that she wanted to see the sun go down at midnight into the sea . . . So, by the time Vera came scrambling back, it was agreed. Vera, of course, had to be taken into the secret, because she slept in the same room.

They arranged it for the following night.

Dave went far too early and had to stroll round the quiet avenues to kill time. The girls had shown him a gap in the palings, told him where the ladder was kept, pointed out their first-floor balcony at the side of the house . . . When the time came it was child's play. Though it was odd, he thought, as he sneaked through the lilac-bushes, acting Romeo and Juliet in broad daylight.

Sonya was waiting. She peeped down over the carved wooden balustrade, flushed, bright-eyed. Vera hovered in the background. He could hear her suppressed giggles, and Sonya breathlessly imploring her to be silent.

Up went the ladder. Down came Sonya. Her hand stretched out for his, he gripped it reassuringly, then, as she stepped to the ground, he let go again so that he had both hands for the ladder, to swing it quickly out of sight under the lilacs. They did not exchange a word until they were safely through the gap in the fence and across the bridge.

'This is fun!' she admitted.

At this late hour the outermost island was deserted except for a few young couples like themselves. Someone in the green shadows, down by the water's edge, was plucking at a balalaika. The plaintive air was the one thing needed to complete the enchantment of the place.

No one else seemed seriously interested in the sunset. They had the rocky little promontory to themselves. Dave had brought a flask of coffee, chocolate and crackers, rare delicacies obtained from the Embassy for this special occasion. They had a midnight picnic as the sun dallied on the rim of the green sea.

'It is lovely,' she murmured.

'Be honest – you're glad you came?'

'Of course, Dave!'

It grew chilly. He felt her shiver. He put his jacket round her shoulders. She protested. 'But *you* will be cold!'

'Not me!'

'In any case we must be going back.'

'A few more minutes!'

'But, Dave, if the School found out! It could be very serious.' She turned her face, pale now in the gloaming, her great eyes luminous. 'What if they expelled me?'

He snorted disbelievingly. 'They wouldn't!'

'Why not?'

'For breaking a silly little rule? You're too good a dancer.'

That pleased her. 'You think I *am* good, Dave? Really?'

'Sure!'

'But how much do you understand of ballet?'

'I know this much – you come to the States, one day, and you'll knock 'em cold!'

' "Knock 'em cold"?' she echoed. 'Oh, Dave, you are sweet!'

But he could not persuade her to stay out any longer. They hurried back through the twilit groves and found the ladder just where they had left it. The house was silent and unlit. No one seemed to have discovered her absence. 'Thank God!' she murmured, and, as they said their hasty good-night, he could feel the flutter of her heart.

It was a long walk home to the Pension but he could have danced all the way, his own heart was so light. The sleeping city was magical at this hour. The Neva rolled silently beneath its bridges, faintly phosphorescent. The palaces stood up proudly, ethereal under the greyly marbled sky. The squares stretched away like deserts, empty save for an obelisk or statue, some bygone emperor in bronze, gigantic on a rearing steed. The canals were streaks of silver in canyons of looming shadow.

Why waste time in sleep, when this beauty would so soon be over?

He was leg-weary, but mentally alert still when he reached the Pension. Yasha opened the door. The *dvornik* was always deferential – no one tipped better than the young Amerikansky – but tonight there was an insolent look in his red-rimmed eyes. He reeked of cheap liquor. He touched his cap and slouched back to his den.

Dave climbed the stairs quietly, fumbling for his key.

He had learnt to slip into the Pension without waking anyone. Linda could sleep through anything after a hard day at the hospital, Anton was doing some rush job at *Pravda* tonight, but Madame and Miss Upton slept the light sleep of the elderly and were easily disturbed.

So he slid the key into the outer door of the apartment and opened it inch by inch with the utmost delicacy.

Immediately he was aware of something strange. At the far end of the hallway someone was talking in a low, excited voice.

Someone, in fact, was on the telephone, despite the unusual hour. Dave stopped in his tracks, not meaning to eavesdrop, only anxious not to interrupt.

The voice was Zorin's. It was muffled, as though his hand was cupped round the mouthpiece, so that the sound would not penetrate to the bedrooms.

'You should find Lenin at the Party headquarters,' he was saying. 'Kamenev you will catch when you raid the *Pravda* building.'

Dave, waiting considerately on the threshold, the door ajar, could not help hearing. And having heard, the final phrase especially, he froze where he was and listened unashamedly.

'Never mind about the warrants,' Zorin continued impatiently. 'There is no time for legal scruples. I tell you, you must act tonight . . . Yes . . . This Bolshevik business must be nipped in the bud . . . If they offer resistance, so much the better! Then you have every excuse . . . No need for white gloves!' He chuckled. Dave did not like the sound. It was somehow different from the genial chuckle he had always associated with the man. 'A phrase of Lenin's,' he was explaining to the unknown person at the other end of the line. 'Serve him right to turn it against

him. As for *Pravda*, the rougher your men are the better.
The paper mustn't come out again. Your men will know
what to do ... Right ... Then let action commence! At
once. As agreed. At once.'

He must not meet Zorin. Zorin must not know that he
had overheard.

Dave stepped back on to the landing. He closed the
door as carefully as he had opened it and drew out his key
without the faintest click.

Something very odd, very ugly, was going on. He must
warn Anton.

Yasha looked sullen when he had to unbolt the door
again. 'All young men are mad,' he growled.

CHAPTER SEVENTEEN

Dawn Raid

Now suddenly the silvery gloaming was no longer beautiful. It was full of danger.

Dave ran, lightly but purposefully, his feet flying over the cobbles.

The telephone would have been quicker. But Zorin barred him from the Pension telephone and he could think of nowhere open at this hour where he could make a call to Anton's office.

The only thing was to go there himself. He could do it in a quarter of an hour or so. He should, with luck, be in time.

What had Zorin said? 'The rougher your men are the better. The paper mustn't come out again. Your men will know what to do . . .'

What men? On whose side, for goodness sake, did Zorin stand?

Was it possible, after all, that he was a police spy, had been all along, as one of Anton's fellow-prisoners had suggested? Obviously he was not a genuine Bolshevik. He must have been keeping up an elaborate pretence, incredibly patient, month after month, maybe year after year. Well, it had paid off. He had been one of the party welcoming Lenin at the station, so he must have wormed himself into the inner councils of the Bolshevik movement.

Dave had heard of such cases. The Ochrana was said to plant its agents like that. He found it hard to believe of the plump, good-natured Zorin. He didn't *look* like a police spy. But then he didn't look like a Bolshevik either. Successful spies never did look like spies. Only tonight, in the silence of the flat, thinking himself the only person awake, had Zorin betrayed his real personality.

There was a clatter of hoofs approaching. Dave flung himself into a doorway. A file of Cossacks trotted by, grey and shadowy. The pale light glinted on their sword-hilts and carbines, on the rows of cartridges slanting across their chests.

They passed. He hurried on, his breath coming in sobs. He heard a truck rattling over the paved roadway. Again he dived for cover before it came lurching round the corner, packed with armed men.

Clearly, something was happening tonight. Zorin's friends were going into action. Zorin had said, 'at once'.

At least the parties he had seen had been headed in the opposite direction. If the Bolsheviks were to be surprised and crushed, their enemies had to strike in several places at once: the headquarters at Kshesinskaya's palace, the *Pravda* offices, the homes of local leaders ... With luck, he might reach Anton in time.

'No need for white gloves ...' He winced at the memory of Zorin's cold-blooded tone.

All right, maybe Anton had asked for it, getting mixed up with these folks ... Maybe it *had* been Lenin who had said it first ... That did not make Dave any less keen to save his friend.

Thank God, there was no sign of anything unusual outside the *Pravda* building! A truck, one or two battered old automobiles, a motor-cycle that he recognized as a

Triumph – a British Army machine that must have been sent to Russia during the war – all these were lined up outside, part of the ramshackle fleet of vehicles used to distribute the paper to the outlying suburbs.

As he approached the entrance he could hear the thunder of the presses within. Everything was still normal.

The doorman asked his business. Luckily Dave had called for Anton once before. It was the same man, and he had not forgotten the American boy.

'You know your way, comrade? Editorial – the second floor.'

Dave turned, his foot on the bottom stair. 'This place is going to be raided – you'd better warn the editor or someone! I don't know who – police or Cossacks or someone. They'll be here any minute now.'

The man started towards him, amazed, stammering questions. But Dave was not going to be delayed – he'd told all he knew and he'd got to find Anton. He raced up the uncarpeted stairs three at a time.

Anton had just cleared his desk and was wriggling his arms into his jacket.

'Dave! This is a pleasant surprise!'

'The next one won't be!' said Dave tersely. 'There's a whole bunch of fellows coming to break up this place. Come on!'

'Is this a joke?' Dave's grim face was the most convincing answer. 'But how do you know this?' Anton demanded.

'I heard Zorin on the telephone. That guy's no more a Bolshevik than I am. He's double-crossed you.'

'I – I cannot believe it! Zorin?'

'Will you stop arguing? I told the doorman – I just hope he passed the warning on—'

'Listen! The presses have stopped!'

The building no longer shook with the vibration from the machine-room below. Instead, there was now a rumble of human voices. Then came a revolver-shot, followed by a second and a third.

'Do you believe me now?' Dave shouted. 'Come on, you got to get out of here!' He almost dragged Anton into the corridor. 'Isn't there a back staircase or something?'

There were no more shots. But there was a wild hubbub below, crashes and bangs mingled with yells and cursing.

Anton started for the rear of the building, then wheeled round. He was white to the lips. 'No – no, Dave! The comrades are fighting down there – I must go and join them—'

'The comrades are being beaten up,' Dave corrected him grimly. 'You've nothing to fight with. These other guys have pistols. And axes by the sound of it.' He peered down the well of the main staircase. 'And looks like they're taking prisoners. It's no good, Anton. Don't waste yourself. They'll be up here too in a minute. Be sensible,' he pleaded.

'Very well.' Anton led the way down a narrow corridor. 'There is a time to resist – and a time to go underground.'

Even at a moment like this Anton talked as though he were quoting.

They met no one, though several doors stood open and there were lights on, as though the staff had rushed out at the first alarm. A telephone was ringing, unanswered.

The two boys hurtled down the back stairs. Through a window Dave saw the dawn pink above the rooftops. At ground level he caught a glimpse into the machine-room. Men were battering the presses with axes and sledge-hammers. The workshop was in chaos, the floor strewn with type and trampled papers. The printing staff had given up the hopeless struggle. Some were being dragged away.

'Quick!' said Anton hoarsely. 'Through the yard.'

Someone was bawling at them from a window above. Dave was more than ever convinced that they should get away, and far away, before the premises were sealed off.

Was it already too late? Anton peered stealthily out into the street. He promptly drew back his head.

'It is no use, Dave. There are scores of these men. And I can see Cossacks further down the street.'

Dave took a peep for himself. Men were being stopped and questioned, some arrested.

He also saw the British motor-cycle, propped against the wall, not thirty yards away. An idea came.

'Can you ride a motor-bike?' he whispered.

'I? No!'

'Then you must trust me. I've ridden my cousin's a few times. If I can get the thing started, I shall wheel it round this way. Keep out of sight till I'm level with you – then run out and jump on the back. But for Pete's sake mind how you do it – if you make me wobble I'll fall off. Okay?'

'Okay!'

Dave marched out with a quietly confident air he was far from feeling. Halfway to the motor-cycle he was stopped by an unpleasant-looking man waving a pistol. '*Amerikansky!*' said Dave, and waved his papers in return. The man with the pistol advised him to get out, and quickly. This was no place for foreigners.

'Just as soon as I can,' said Dave under his breath, adding a silent prayer that he could start the machine. He'd never been on a Triumph in his life. He seized the handlebars, kicked the starter, and felt a surge of joy as the engine roared. He was in the saddle ... He was

wheeling in the roadway ... Men were shouting to him
to stop, leaping aside when he didn't ...

Anton came out of the side-entrance like a shell from a
gun. Dave thought they were done for as the other boy
hurled himself on to the carrier, his fingers clutching frantically, his feet groping for a resting-place. The motor-cycle
wavered and almost toppled over. Somehow Dave righted
it, accelerated, and went roaring down the street. A
Cossack rode at them, sabre raised, but his horse reared
in panic at the racket made by the engine, and they were
out of danger before he could regain control. A carbine
cracked, a bullet splintered a flagstone in front ... 'Lean
left on the corner!' Dave shouted 'I'm turning!' Anton, for
once, obeyed without argument. They managed the turn
without disaster and were hidden from their pursuers.

Dave did not stop until they had gone a couple of
miles. They were somewhere in the outer suburbs. Factory
chimneys stood up against the red sky, trailing lazy pen-
nants of smoke. Dave put his foot down and glanced
round. There was no sign of pursuit.

'Now what?' he asked.

Anton was still bemused. It had all happened in a quarter of an hour.

'I – I don't understand, Dave. You said something
about Zorin?'

Dave explained what little he knew. Anton boiled with
indignation. Zorin! The snake! No punishment could be
bad enough for such a traitor—

Dave had to stem the flow. 'The point is, where do you
go from here? Is it safe to go back to the Pension? Will
they be looking for you personally?'

Anton considered. 'I doubt that. I am not important
enough. I am not a Party member.'

'But Zorin knows you work for *Pravda*.'

'True. I had better lie low, as you say, until the whole position clarifies. I will telephone you tomorrow night. You will indicate how things stand at your end.'

'Sure.'

It seemed safest to abandon the motor-cycle then and there, and separate. Anton had friends to go to. His one worry was about the motor-cycle.

'It is not ours,' he said with furrowed brow. 'I do not know whose it is.'

Dave laughed. 'You'll never make a Bolshevik,' he said, 'if you worry so much about private property.'

That day there were raids on Bolshevik premises all over the city. *Pravda* was closed down, its editor, Kamenev hauled off to jail. The biggest fish, Lenin, escaped the net, along with Zinoviev and several of the leaders. Some said he was hiding in the forest outside the city, others that he had been spirited away in a German submarine. Trotsky defiantly invited arrest: he preferred to face his enemies. Otherwise, the chief Bolsheviks were already in prison or in hiding.

'*The Provisional Govenment is getting tough at last,*' Dave wrote. '*Kerensky is taking over as Prime Minister, he is still going to be Minister of War as well. I've heard him speak, he's a mighty fine orator, more like an actor almost. But you tell me always to look for the hard facts, not the words, and I guess the facts are hard enough for him, right now. The war isn't going so well again.*'

That was an understatement. In fact, the offensive had petered out, the Germans had launched a massive counter-attack, and the Russian armies were crumbling into rout.

But the full seriousness of the disaster had not yet filtered through to the public.

At the Pension there was some concern when Anton did not come home. Dave privately reassured Madame. He merely told her that Anton had escaped the *Pravda* raid and was staying with friends. She did not press him with questions. So long as Anton was safe, she preferred not to know any compromising details.

It was hard to sit calmly at dinner with Zorin. The man looked tired but pleased with himself. Otherwise he was the same deceptively genial character as ever.

'You have had a hard day's business?' Dave inquired politely.

'So-so, my boy.'

When Miss Upton set out her ludo-board, Zorin went off to his room. An hour later he poked his head round the door. 'I am just going to the post, Madame. I shall be back before you serve the tea.'

On a sudden impulse Dave leapt up and followed him into the hallway. 'May I take your letter for you, Mr Zorin?'

'Thank you, no. I like the evening air.'

'But isn't it dangerous for you? To show yourself on the streets? When they are arresting so many Bolsheviks?'

Zorin shrugged his shoulders. 'Oh, I am not so well known, my boy. I work in the background. I have always covered my tracks pretty well.'

'I guess you have.' With a lightning gesture Dave tweaked the letter from his hand. Zorin swore and snatched it back, but not before Dave had read the address. It was to police headquarters.

'What do you think you are doing?' snarled Zorin. He

faced Dave in the hallway. He looked suddenly dangerous. They both kept their voices down.

'I know what *you* are doing. You see – I heard you on the 'phone last night. I was standing there, with the door ajar. I got to the *Pravda* offices just in time to warn Anton.'

'You little devil!' Zorin went pale. His breath came heavily. 'You mean – you told him all you heard?'

'You bet! And he didn't much like it.'

'Where is he now?'

'Do you think I'd tell you – if I knew? He has other friends in this city.'

Zorin seemed to have shrunk, like a teddy bear that had lost its stuffing. Without another word he turned and ran up to his room. There were noises of hasty packing. Within a few minutes he came down again, his winter overcoat draped over his shoulders though it was mid-July, his bulging suitcase in his hand. He marched into the living-room and, under the astonished eyes of the three ladies, laid a handful of grubby paper roubles in front of Madame.

'My apologies,' he said thickly. 'I am called away suddenly. Business. No, I cannot leave an address.'

He shook hands all round. Not quite all round. Dave managed to avoid the farewells. Instead, as he held open the door, he murmured: 'Sure there's no address? But I guess your old Party comrades will know where to find you?'

That thought did not seem to bring comfort to Zorin. He rushed out of the apartment as if invisible pursuers were already on his heels.

CHAPTER EIGHTEEN

'All Power to the Soviets'

Anton came back the next day, rather jaunty after his adventure.

'Zorin was wise to make himself scarce!' he declared. 'No matter. Justice will overtake him.'

'Maybe,' said Dave. 'But that kind of guy knows how to look after himself. They have a knack of coming out on the right side, whoever wins.'

Anton shrugged. 'At least we have solved one mystery – we know now who listened at the door on the first night you came here.'

'Sure. And we can do without his sort hanging around. Do you think he'll report on you to the Ochrana?'

'I think not. The Government cannot jail every Bolshevik, let alone mere sympathisers like me. It is a pity I have lost my work – but it is for the moment only. The Bolsheviks will be back. History is on their side.'

Dave couldn't see it. Anton was delighted to explain.

The German philosopher, Karl Marx, had foretold it all years ago. Sooner or later the working-classes of the world would rise up, overthrow their masters, and establish communism. That would be the end of war, poverty and oppression. Marx had been wrong about one thing only: he had not expected the revolution to start in Russia.

'But it is going to!' cried Anton exultantly. 'We Russians

have that honour. Already we have got rid of the Tsar. Now we must sweep away Kerensky. We shall make our own revolution, a true revolution, and the rest of the world will follow.'

'You make it sound easy,' said Dave dryly. 'But how many Russians have even heard of this guy Marx – isn't he dead and buried, anyways?'

'Lenin and the other Bolsheviks carry on his message!'

'Only they're locked up – or daren't show their faces. Honestly, Anton, how big a following have they? Do they really amount to that much? I'm sorry – I just can't see them licking a government, even a tottery one like this.'

'No? I will show you. At this moment there is one big power, one big organization only, that you can compare with the Provisional Government?'

'The Soviets? Sure.' Dave nodded. Since the spring uprising, the committees of soldiers, sailors and workmen had become more and more important. They alone really had the confidence of the masses. They had established themselves in the Smolny Institute, a former high-class girls' school not far from the Tauride Palace. The Soviets were almost like a rival to the Government, which they continually criticized. They were far too strong for Kerensky to suppress. 'But the Soviets aren't Bolshevik,' Dave objected. 'They are made up of all sorts.'

'Lenin will work through them.'

Anton picked up a wooden doll that Dave had just bought to send home to his small sister. It was a typical piece of peasant toymaking – a plump, brightly-painted figure, that took apart to reveal another smaller doll inside, with a diminutive third doll inside that.

'I will illustrate,' said Anton. He held up the big doll. 'This represents the Soviets.' He unscrewed the top half and lifted out the next doll. 'This is the whole Socialist group – Mensheviks, Bolsheviks, what you will. They hold many different opinions. Even the Bolsheviks dispute among themselves.'

'You must enjoy that,' said Dave, checking a smile.

'I am not in their private discussions,' said Anton seriously, 'but I know it is so. No matter.' He produced the innermost doll. 'Here, in the very centre, you have Lenin and those who agree with him. They are the ones who know what they want and how to get it.' Anton fitted the dolls together again, one inside another. 'That is how it will be,' he said.

Anton's confident forecast was hard to swallow in July. By September the picture was different.

General Kornilov, who had now been made commander-in-chief of the armies at the front, fell out with Kerensky and began to move troops against the capital. There was a week of frenzied rumours. The Cossack general was going to set himself up as a dictator. Every one must unite against him, to defend the liberty that Russia had so newly won.

Kerensky could fight only one enemy at a time. Kornilov seemed more dangerous than the Bolsheviks. Indeed, Kornilov could not be beaten without the help of the Bolsheviks: through the Soviets, they wielded so much influence among the rank-and-file soldiers and the workers. So the prison-doors had to be opened. The arrested Bolshevik leaders were set free, the charges dropped. Others came out of hiding. But not Lenin. No one knew what had happened to the bald little man with the glinting eyes. Was he dead? Or in Germany? Or just biding his time?

'*For once,*' Dave told his father, '*the people here seem to be united: they don't mean Kornilov to lead his Cossacks into Petersburg.*'

He had seen the workmen pouring from the factories, demanding rifles and getting them. He had seen the barricades going up in the main streets. He had seen the tough-looking sailors arriving from Kronstadt, mingling with the soldiers and the cloth-capped volunteers.

'And we have comrades elsewhere,' boasted Anton. 'The railwaymen are with us. Kornilov cannot move armies quickly except by train. But locomotives can be put out of order, tracks can be torn up, signals can be jammed! All this is being done – but not because Kerensky says so. Because the Soviets say so!'

'*What it amounts to,*' Dave wrote home, '*is that there are getting to be two governments: the official one, Kerensky and his ministers, and this set-up of working-class committees that they call the Soviets.*'

The Soviets even had their contacts with Kornilov's advancing armies. Those armies never came within gun-shot of the capital. Soviet agitators met the advance-guard, talked with the soldiers and won them over. Kornilov's power melted away. There was mutiny everywhere. Some of his generals were arrested by their own troops, who elected delegates and sent them off to Petersburg to get instructions from the Soviets. At last Kornilov himself was arrested. His counter-revolution collapsed.

'Kerensky thinks he has saved us,' said Anton. 'It is not so. The Soviets defeated Kornilov. Kerensky thinks he is on top of the world. He is a fool. He has given the workers rifles and now he cannot take them back. He has let the Bolsheviks out of jail and he cannot lock them up again.'

It was lucky for the Russians, thought Dave, that their country was so vast. For all this time, while they struggled among themselves, the Germans were remorselessly gnawing further and further eastwards. They had just taken the Baltic port of Riga. If the Russian armies continued to dissolve into mutiny and mass-desertion, how long would even Petersburg be safe?

Miss Upton had given up sticking flags into her map. It was all too confusing and depressing. She did not know what had come over the world.

Summer was dead. The green trees turned golden brown and yellow. Their leaves fluttered sadly down.

Yelagin Island was desolate, the avenues bare like brooms against the greying skies. But Dave no longer walked there. The Ballet School had shut up its summer hostel by the bridge. In any case, Sonya had triumphantly passed her finals and signed her new contract. She was a student no more, but a junior member of the company. She could live where she pleased. So she was back with her grandmother, and her talkative friend Vera was installed in Zorin's old room. The Pension Yalta was gay and youthful again. There were midnight suppers when the girls had been performing.

'Great heavens!' Anton would exclaim in despair, when he came home, inky-fingered and weary from the office – *Pravda* was in full production once more. 'So much happening in our country, so much happening in the world! And you can think of nothing but arabesques and pirouettes and how many curtains Karsavina took last night! Life is passing by – and you are seeing nothing!'

Vera would go into fits of giggles. Sonya would fix her great eyes upon him and answer quietly:

'Foolish boy, it is only art that gives meaning to life.'

'Girls!' Anton would groan. 'What can you do with them, Dave?'

'They're all right,' said Dave.

'Thank you.' Sonya gave him a radiant smile. 'You understand!' His spirits rose.

Soon afterwards, he started a letter to his father. He wrote home mostly once a week, but each letter was put together in spare moments. Sometimes it was like a diary.

'*I have been thinking over what you say about coming home,*' he scribbled. '*I know we said a year, but I think after all it might be worth staying on a bit longer. Winter's a bad time to travel.*' He scratched his head, searching for more excuses. '*I should not like Mom to worry too much about my getting torpedoed crossing the Atlantic – maybe we shall have the Germans licked by spring.*' He pondered and went on. '*And nothing worse seems likely to happen in this city. Leastways, Mr Francis reckons the Bolsheviks have missed their chance and won't be able to make a second revolution – I met him on the Embassy steps last week, and he stopped and asked after you, and sent you his cordial greetings.*'

Dave re-read the last few lines and wondered if he was being quite honest with his parents. It was true, of course. Mr Francis had said just that, and surely an ambassador should know more about these things than a boy?

He folded the paper and put it back in his pocket, to be continued later. There was a defiant look in his eyes.

He wasn't leaving Russia till Dad sent the kind of order he wouldn't dare to disobey.

The autumn was passing. Rain rolled in from the Gulf, the side-roads turned to mud, the paved squares collected puddles like lakes, mirroring the anxious palaces.

When there was no rain there was fog. It wreathed down the narrower streets, hung its curtains across the pewter-grey Neva, hid the long vistas of the Nevsky Prospect. Dave recalled his arrival in St Petersburg. The year's wheel had almost turned full circle.

There was a fog inside his mind, too. He could not see ahead: it was just like groping his way down the ill-lit Nevsky. He tried to take an intelligent interest in what was happening, but it was so difficult to find out.

Lenin had come back, Anton confided importantly. He had been hiding not far away in Finland. Now, clean-shaven, a wig covering his baldness, forged identity papers in his pocket, he flitted through the dark city and reappeared in the secret inner councils of the Bolsheviks.

Two forces glowered at each other across the city, each in its stronghold.

Kerensky and his ministers carried on the government from the Winter Palace – still tried, indeed, to carry on the war against Germany and to keep faith with their western allies. But hardly anyone else in Russia now believed in the war. Too many millions had died in the mud and snow. Too many were starving and desperate. 'Peace and bread!' was the cry.

Two or three miles away, where the river made its great bend at the eastern edge of St Petersburg, the Soviets had turned the Smolny Institute into a citadel of their own.

Armed sentries checked passes at the doors. Former classrooms and teachers' common-rooms were now offices and meeting-places for innumerable committees. Somewhere, in one of those hundred rooms, sat Lenin's old rival, now his uneasy ally, the mercurial Trotsky – with his flashing eyes and fiery oratory, his mane of black hair, his dapper dress and expressive manicured hands, the complete opposite of the Bolshevik leader. But at this hour they were working for the same objective. Lenin was hammering out the manifestos and the slogans: and Trotsky, as chairman the Military Revolutionary Committee, was planning the seizure of key-points and the placing of machine-guns, the taking over of an empire that had lost its emperor but still covered one-sixth of the earth.

One day Anton rushed in excitedly and announced to the whole dinner-table:

'Kerensky is showing his true colours – he has come out as the petty tyrant he really is!'

'Sit down,' said Madame, 'and eat your dinner.'

'I can stay only a few minutes – I must go back. The office is in a state of siege.' Anton attacked his bowl of cabbage soup. 'Kerensky is trying to destroy free speech. He turned the staff out of the building and had the doors sealed. But Trotsky sent us troops – they broke the seals – we are back at work again – and the soldiers are protecting us!'

'It sounds to me highly illegal,' said Miss Upton.

'You're heading for jail again,' said Linda cheerfully.

Anton snorted. 'We have gone past that point,' he mumbled through a mouthful of bread. 'Kerensky has declared war on democracy. He has rushed off to find troops who will support him – he is going to bring them back to

Petersburg and suppress the Soviets! Or so he thinks. He hasn't a hope.'

'Dear God,' said Madame with a heavy sigh. 'More fighting!'

'There is only one way to stop the fighting for good and all.' Anton jumped up, wiping his lips. 'We must sweep away Kerensky's government before he can return. The answer now is: "All power to the Soviets!" '

CHAPTER NINETEEN

At the Winter Palace

Even now it was hard to get the two dancers to realize that anything unusual was happening.

'The shops are all open,' said Vera. 'Not that there's anything in them,' she added wistfully.

'The street-cars are running in the Nevsky,' said Sonya. 'People are lining up outside the cinemas. Of *course* we must report at the theatre as usual. They will never cancel the performance.'

'I should hope not!' cried Vera.

When it was time to go, Dave escorted them. The streets were seething with Red Guards, soldiers and sailors from the *Aurora*, the cruiser that Kerensky (said Anton) had ordered to sea, because he did not trust its pro-Bolshevik crew. Either the vessel hadn't gone, or these men had deserted.

'There will be empty seats tonight,' said Vera resentfully. 'Some people will never get through this mob – or they will be too nervous to come out at all. What a shame! Would you like to see the ballet again, Dave? I'm sure we could get you a pass.'

Any other time Dave would have accepted with gratitude. Tonight, however, there was something in the air. Even with Sonya dancing, he felt he could not sit still in a theatre. He declined Vera's offer, promised to collect them after the final curtain, and strode away into the darkness.

It looked as though the Soviet supporters had by now gained control of most of the city. No police, no Government troops seemed to be challenging the red-armleted workmen as they surged to and fro on their unknown missions. He wondered if there was any chance of telephoning Anton, or whether the *Pravda* offices were cut off. He knew that Kerensky had earlier managed to cut off the lines serving the Soviet headquarters at the Smolny, and they had had to improvise a corps of motor-cyclists instead.

He turned into the ornate entrance of the Europe, the luxury hotel on the corner of the Nevsky, where he had long ago discovered that his American appearance – and his American dollars – ensured him a warm welcome. Tonight, the atmosphere like the lighting was subdued. There was no sign of the officers and flashy business men who could usually be found drinking champagne even at the most critical moments. The porter who conducted him to the telephone actually hesitated and glanced round nervously before pocketing his tip.

'They say we are not to, in future, *barin* . . . it is against the spirit of the Revolution. God help us all!'

Dave got through to the *Pravda* offices quite quickly and Anton came on the line.

'You just caught me in time,' he said.

'I was surprised to get you at all.'

'Why? We hold the telephone exchange.'

'You do?'

'And the railway stations. In fact, most of the key places. Except the Winter Palace itself. I'm going there now.'

'*You* are? The Winter Palace? I thought you just said—'

'Yes, the so-called Government is holding out there. We may have to carry the place by storm.'

Anton's voice sounded high-pitched over the wire. Dave could picture his face at the other end, eyes burning, hair electric with heroic idealism.

'But – you're not a soldier,' he protested weakly. 'You're not even a Red Guard—'

'I have a pistol,' retorted Anton. 'I must take my place with the others at the barricades.'

'Listen, Anton, don't do anything crazy—'

The line had gone dead.

As he hung up the receiver, Dave heard the boom of a distant gun. It was like the midday cannon, but it was not midday, and the shot had not come from the Fortress of St Peter and St Paul.

The porter stood ashen-faced, rubbing his hands. 'That shot, *barin*! It was from the cruiser – she is anchored in the river. The scoundrels are going to bombard the Winter Palace!'

The night crackled with occasional shots. Now and again there was the muffled crump of an exploding shell.

Dave turned westwards along the Nevsky. The great thoroughfare ran arrow-straight to the heart of the city, to the Winter Palace and the Admiralty. He hurried, not at all clear why, but feeling that he must get there as soon as possible.

A Red Guard challenged him but let him pass. Another quarter of a mile brought him within sight of the Palace, its long façade rising, oddly unreal and like a theatre set, beyond the empty expanse of square. The lights were burning in the windows. The Palace stretched its brilliant length like a peace-time liner.

There were barricades, here, improvised from loads of firewood, an abandoned car, torn-up paving-stones. There was a wheeled machine-gun, surrounded by muttering soldiers. Men with rifles lurked in doorways and porticoes, peering out across the square. For a moment the firing had died down.

A workman with a cartridge-belt slung over one shoulder put his hand on Dave's arm. Everyone was friendly enough, once Dave opened his mouth and betrayed his nationality. It was only each other that these Russians seemed to distrust.

'You can go no further – you might be shot.'

'What is happening?'

'The people in there won't surrender. We shall have to pull them out by the ears. We thought the shells would bring them to their senses. But no. Now we wait for orders. We don't want to destroy the Palace.'

'Is the Government in there?'

'The old gang, yes. All but Kerensky himself. And they have troops – officer-cadets mostly – the kind that won't come over to our side. It won't be easy. You had better go back, Amerikansky. You might get hurt – and this is not your quarrel.'

Dave saw that there was no hope of finding Anton in these conditions. The Palace itself was so huge – it covered four or five acres – and the cordon of besiegers stretched round it was correspondingly long. Nor was there any clear organization, no one knew where any-body else was, or who was in charge. Each barricade, each patrol, was a little world of its own.

At least the shelling had ceased and the rifle-fire had

dwindled to a casual shot at long intervals. But the bombardment began again about eleven, just as Dave was taking the girls home from the theatre. He was lucky enough to find a taxi, and they drove a roundabout way through the side-streets to avoid the barricades.

'Those are the Peter-Paul batteries,' the driver told them. 'They are firing straight across the river at the Palace.'

No one at the Pension thought of going to bed.

Sonya, usually ravenous after a performance, could scarcely swallow her supper. She roved from room to room, her eyes round with foreboding.

'Anton – the idiot! Listen to those guns! He will be blown to pieces!'

Linda tried to soothe her with reasonable arguments. Anton was on the same side as the guns, they were not firing at *him*.

'But the Palace is full of young officers! You know what they are like. They will fight to the death. Anton is just the boy to go charging at them, waving a red flag or something absurd – and they will shoot him down like a dog!'

No one knew what to answer. Sonya had summed it up all too vividly. Despite his past few months' association with the unsentimental Bolsheviks, Anton had never changed, deep down. He remained the romantic idealist, ever eager to find a hero's grave. There was a real danger, tonight, that he would do so.

Some time after midnight they realized that the grumble of gunfire had died away. Vera stood up with a yawn.

'Come on, Sonya. We have rehearsals tomorrow.'

'No!' said Sonya violently. 'I am going to see what has happened.'

She ran out into the hallway, seized her coat, and stooped to take her galoshes from the row standing by the door.

'But Sonya! *Rehearsals*!' Vera looked aghast. 'What will the Director—'

'Devil take the Director!'

Dave knew there was no stopping her. 'Hold on,' he said. 'I'll go with you.' Linda said she was coming too. Vera shrugged her shoulders and let them go.

The siege, such as it was, had ended.

The barricades lay unguarded and abandoned. Rifles and cartridge-belts were strewn about, as if no longer required. The stately façade of the Winter Palace was flood-lit by a number of searchlights. Dave could see little sign of damage.

Sonya led them across the square, almost running. The Palace loomed in front of them, armed men trickling in and out of the wide-open doors. Dave felt the broken glass crunch under his feet as they drew near. Fragments of stucco littered the ground like crumbs from some giant iced cake. There was a dismantled barricade. A sailor sat on it, calmly winding a red-spattered bandage round his leg.

Sonya paused to ask him: 'Are there many casualties?'

'A few dozen. They soon caved in when they heard the shells whistling over their heads!'

'Come on!' she gasped to the others.

At the entrance a Red Guard barred the way. Who were they? What business—. But Dave recognized a young

American journalist, John Reed, and they were able to tag along behind his party.

The vaulted entrance-hall echoed like a railway terminus. Bewildered flunkeys, still resplendent in the old imperial uniform of red, blue and gold, waved ineffectual arms and stammered polite prohibitions that everyone ignored. The common people, tonight, had taken over the seats of the mighty.

Magnificent stairways, ornate corridors, branched off in various directions. Huge gilded mirrors doubled the long vistas, tricked the eye with a repetition of images. Crystal chandeliers dangled from the lofty ceilings, arrogant portraits looked down upon the cloth-capped conquerers slowly pushing their way through the galleries. Here and there, through a shattered window, blew a draught of night air, cold as reality.

There had been some hand-to-hand fighting. There were bullet-marks, stains on the floor, overturned furniture. Two or three men were carried past on stretchers: Dave craned to see their faces, but none resembled Anton. A group of cadets, prisoners, were herded through, white and grim.

The three friends elbowed their way forward, scanning the crowds in each apartment as they reached it. Some looting had begun. Dave saw a workman seize a bronze clock. A soldier had decorated his cap with ostrich plumes. Other men were protesting. 'Comrades, don't touch anything! It's the property of the People now!'

Still no sign of Anton . . .

'He must be here,' said Sonya.

They found themselves in a great room in the heart of the Palace, hung with crimson brocade, gleaming with gold and coppery-green malachite. There was a long baize-covered table, set out for a meeting, with pen and paper laid in front of each vacant chair. Here, one of the Bolsheviks explained to them exultantly, the gentlemen of the Provisional Government had still been sitting, drafting their useless orders and proclamations, when the besiegers rushed in. They were now on their way to the cells in the Peter-Paul Fortress, he added. No, nobody had been hurt.

Sonya turned, weaving her way through the gaping crowd with demonic determination. There were still miles of corridors, it seemed, acres of state apartments in this glittering labyrinth.

'We shall never find him,' panted Linda. 'Talk about a needle in a haystack—'

And certainly they never *would* have found Anton, but just then there was a shout that was taken up and echoed from room to room: 'All out! Everybody outside!' There was an immediate movement towards the stairs. Red Guards were repeating: 'All out! No looting, comrades! We are not bandits!'

Dave and the girls were caught up in a slow current of shuffling humanity that spiralled downstairs and out through a back door opening on to the Neva embankment. Two armleted men with revolvers stood confiscating any loot they detected. A third man sat at a table, listing the items as they were handed in.

And just outside, in the dank night, stood Anton, indignantly clamouring to be let in again. A sentry pushed him away good-humouredly. 'No, comrade! The order is "all out"!'

When he saw his friends, Anton gave up arguing. He greeted them with amazed delight.

'You here? Isn't it wonderful! Complete victory! A clean sweep! And – you'll never guess – that snake Zorin was in here too – I saw him taken away—'

'Never mind Zorin!' Sonya's cry was almost a sob. '*You* are safe – what else matters?' She flung her arms round his neck, burying her white face against him, her shoulders quivering.

Dave stood there, suddenly chilled. It wasn't the cold coming up off the river, either. He had his back to the light shining from the Palace. He was glad that nobody could see his face.

So this was how it was! Why hadn't he seen it before? Come to that, Anton had been no smarter. He looked a bit dazed himself.

Dave stood, feeling as if he'd just taken a tremendous body-punch. To right and left the people streamed out of the building behind him, pushed past him chattering, trailed away noisily into the darkness. Yet he had never known such a desolating sense of loneliness.

Linda tugged his sleeve, had to tug again to make him fully aware of her.

'Home, now,' she said in her sensible way. 'Let's lead on. Those two will follow.'

'Okay.'

She slipped her arm into his and they started to walk slowly along the embankment. Behind them they could hear Anton babbling of triumph . . .

'A new world is opening!' he kept saying. 'Within the year we shall see an end to the war, revolutions all over Europe! Nothing can ever be the same again!'

You're right there, thought Dave sombrely. For himself, at any rate, nothing could ever be the same again. Not after seeing Sonya's face as she'd rushed into Anton's arms. Who said she lived only for dancing? How blind could you get?

Linda was talking to him. He couldn't take it in. Had

the Bolsheviks really won, or would Kerensky find troops to back him? Would Lenin be the new leader of Russia? Wasn't it exciting, anyway, to be in the midst of things when history was being made? He guessed that Linda was no more concerned about these things, than, right now, he was himself. She was just rattling on, trying to keep an ordinary conversation going. She was real kind, Linda, she did her best . . . She must be good with the wounded soldiers . . . But it didn't help with his sort of pain, and he couldn't concentrate on what she was saying.

With his free hand he groped in his pocket. He pulled out the letter he had started a few days before, asking his parents' permission to stay on. What was the point now? Whether or not Russia was going communist, with no business prospects for his father . . . ? He couldn't worry about all that stuff tonight. The real reason was quite different. One he could tell to nobody in the world.

He would write another letter in the morning. '*I would like to come home as soon as I can fix transportation. I guess I have learned all I can here . . .*'

He crumpled the old letter into a ball and threw it over the granite parapet. Far below, the black, cruel, beautiful Neva took it, and, chuckling, swirled it down to the sea.